The Vietcong stripped him naked, then tied a wire to his scrotum

Ludlow walked with six soldiers in front and four behind. The group entered a village and shoved the American pilot into a bamboo cage. Then they cut the steel wire but left his hands bound.

Someone jabbed him in the back with a sharp stick. A woman laughed and jabbed again, then a dozen children ran up and poked him until he bled.

Finally a VC stared at Ludlow, spat in the pilot's face and said in broken English, "Your jet kill my brother today. In three more days you wish you not ever born."

"The biggest of all adventure series."
—*San Francisco Examiner*

MACK BOLAN
The Executioner

DON PENDLETON's EXECUTIONER
MACK BOLAN
Skysweeper

A GOLD EAGLE BOOK FROM
WORLDWIDE

TORONTO • NEW YORK • LONDON • PARIS
AMSTERDAM • STOCKHOLM • HAMBURG
ATHENS • MILAN • TOKYO • SYDNEY

First edition September 1984

ISBN 0-373-61069-6

Special thanks and acknowledgment to
Chet Cunningham for his contributions to this work.

Printed in Canada

When a hero reaches the Pearly Gates,
To Saint Peter he will tell
Another warrior reporting, Sir.
I've served my time in Hell.

To all those brave Allied soldiers
who fell on the beaches of Normandy.
They, too, were fighting for justice and freedom.

PROLOGUE

From Mack Bolan's journal:

One on one has been one of my earliest doctrines: chess, arm wrestling, footraces, almost any activity where it works.

That philosophy continues. Maybe I'm an anachronism in a world of superweapons, of scientific battles, of fighting with heat-seeking missiles, of laser-aimed rifles, of tanks with computers that automatically select, track, acquire target and fire.

Perhaps I'm a throwback to the caveman where the combatants fought with clubs. The bigger man with the bigger club usually won, unless the smaller man was stronger or smarter or simply better with a club. I like that.

I've said before that any finger can pull a trigger. A boy of ten who can't read or write and without a family or enough to eat, can trigger a LAW rocket and shoot down a $20,000,000 aircraft. A twelve-year-old girl can fire a machine gun and slaughter innocent shoppers in a Mideastern marketplace. It doesn't take specific training to kill.

The same holds true for anyone behind any weapon. A good tool such as a knife can kill. A good development such as atomic energy can be shifted from progressive scientific benefits for mankind and turned into weapons. What bothers me about this is that any of these devices can and do fall into the wrong hands.

When a misguided soul gets behind an Armageddon-type atomic weapon, only bad things can happen.

No, I don't hate science. It has given us tremendous creature comforts and I appreciate them as much as anyone.

Still I worry.

Yes, I will use a laser-sighted rifle if I have to, and I have used heat-seeking rockets to drive Animal Man back into his sewer.

But too many times I have seen the evil hydra rise up and utilize these same scientific advances for vile purposes.

These savages have no respect for the sanctity of human life. They do not give a second thought to marring civilization with their terror. They are inhuman, brutish cancers on mankind who defile, terrorize, maim and kill to further their diabolical and selfish ends.

When I go into battle one on one with these ghouls, I know my own skills and limitations. I understand what I can and can't do.

A hot firefight, whether in Nam or Lebanon or El Salvador, or in the middle of a headshed's empire in Los Angeles, must be one continuous course of action. There is no time to sit down and logically figure out how to attack a position, or an adversary with a submachine gun.

You act!

Or you die.

When I consider the implications of Animal Man in control of a scientific complex that can literally vaporize four million people by the push of a single button, I pause and shiver. Not from fear, but anger.

I long ago committed myself to this war everlasting with the idea that one day I would pay the supreme price. That's the way of war. I have survived this long through my own skill, with the help of dedicated friends and no small measure of good luck.

But when I go it will be a warrior's death, and even when my body begins to cool, my eyes will still be glaring defiance at the scum who ended my war.

This is a good war.

In good wars good people always die.

1

Mack Bolan sensed a human presence to his left. He pivoted and dived for cover behind the concrete-block wall. He heard a silenced pistol cough twice in the darkness even as he moved, but his early-warning combat antenna had already picked up the danger signal.

The rounds caromed off the masonry and sped harmlessly into the night. Bolan sat up and peered around the base of the blocks, studying the situation.

His gaze took in the large wooden box squatting in the alley. And the Executioner was certain that the sniper—a professional because of the silenced weapon—lay concealed behind the huge crate.

Bolan fisted the sound-suppressed Beretta 93-R, and continued to wait. He knew the gunman had no place to go without showing himself. He had to move sooner or later. When he did he would die.

Bolan had been in this alley in Ridgecrest, California, watching a house, and soon the Executioner realized someone was watching him. The cat-and-mouse game had turned deadly when Bolan decided to deliberately show himself. The other shooter had missed, and sealed his fate.

"Give it up," Bolan shouted. "You've got no-where to go. Buy your life by talking."

The response was two quick rounds from the man behind the heavy wooden crate. Both slugs hit the wall chest high and splattered into the sand. Bolan was crouched well below them. He put one measured shot into the outer edge of the box, sending splinters behind it, but heard no cry of pain.

The gladiators were separated by only thirty feet of sand, and Bolan knew the enemy was getting ready to move out. The Executioner drew his .44 AutoMag just in case he needed it, and laid it on the ground. Then he flicked the 93-R to 3-shot mode and clutched the pistol in a two-handed shooting grip.

Scuffling. Movement!

A blur showed over the box and a form rushed into the open and headed down the alley. Bolan stroked the trigger. The first three slugs blasted the man's legs. Bolan tracked up the muzzle and put three more into the fleeing gunman's side and back. The ambusher had fired one wild shot behind him as he ran, and now his arms were flung outward as his riddled body hurtled headlong into the desert dust and lay still.

The Executioner advanced cautiously, watching the splayed hands, until he was sure the man was dead. Then he holstered the Beretta and dragged the corpse to the box that had hidden him. Bolan dumped the man inside and slid the lid in place. The container that had been his refuge, now became his coffin.

Bolan signaled behind him and a shadow scurried up the alley and crouched beside the Executioner. The man was Dr. Harry Peterson, a physicist and one of the head scientists working on the ultra-top-secret "Skysweeper" laser project for the United States government.

"That man shot at you? Is he dead?"

Mack Bolan turned and glowered at the shadowed face. "We discussed the danger this afternoon, Dr. Peterson."

"Yes, I forgot how my parents said it was. I have forgotten too much about Russia. If my parents weren't still living there, these bastards would have no hold over me. They could never make me do this."

Bolan's rage subsided when he considered the scientist's plight.

The Executioner knew his companion was torn between love for his parents, love for his life's work and patriotism for his adopted country.

Bolan's mind flashed to Pittsfield and his own parents a lifetime ago. The menace remained the same. Only the accent had changed. But whatever cloak the threat wore, the Executioner would see through the disguise. And for Bolan, his quest would always be personal.

"I'll stop them. But if you decide to back down now you can kiss the Skysweeper project goodbye," he told Dr. Peterson. "And there's no telling what they'll do to your parents. Do you want us to continue?"

"Yes. They have made me compromise myself too often already. What do you want me to do?"

Briefly Bolan outlined the plan he had devised.

"Yes. Yes, we must do this now."

Bolan returned to his appraisal of the house. He guessed the modest unit to be about thirty years old. Nondescript, the kind someone working with the KGB would want to use. And Sammy Smith was the kind of treacherous citizen who could be recruited by the resident KGB agent to do his dirty work.

But Bolan had an idea that Smith was more than just small fry. He seemed to have others working for him, and he had some professional protection. Bolan knew the killer he had just snuffed was a KGB field muscle and hit man. It helped even the score, just a little.

Bolan and the physicist lay in the alley for ten minutes watching the back door. No one came or left and the lights were all on. Bolan moved quietly up to the door and rapped twice, then twice again followed by one last knock, as he had seen an earlier caller do. Childish, but Bolan decided to play it that way.

The same man Bolan had seen before at the door opened it and looked out. He was in his forties, with dark hair and a broad face. During his two days in town, Bolan had checked out Smith. He was a lead technician at the China Lake Naval Weapons Center, a huge base where scientists and R & D people tested their inventions. Ridgecrest, the village that had grown up quickly to handle the civilian population, was just over the boundary fence from the military facility.

The man stared blankly at his visitor. "Do I know you?" he asked.

Bolan shook his head. "You may have spoken to me on the phone, but that's all. I control what you do here, however...through others. I would not be here to see you if I was not extremely unhappy with your progress. You told us you could monitor the project from inside. Then why do we not know more about Operation Skysweeper?"

Smith reacted to the shock technique the way Bolan hoped he would. He became flustered, unsure of himself.

"I have brought along one of your people with whom we are also not pleased." Bolan gestured to Dr. Peterson, and the physicist stepped into the light from the door so Smith could see him. "May we come in?" Bolan said.

"Yes, please do. I know Dr. Peterson." They stepped inside and Smith closed the door. "Drink?"

"My American comrade. I did not come here to drink! I came for answers! I want an explanation of exactly where you are in your work."

"Of course, yes." He hesitated and looked pointedly at Dr. Peterson.

"There is no need to worry about Dr. Peterson's loyalty," the Executioner said. "Actually he has been reporting on your performance these past few months."

Smith was sweating, and the Executioner stiffened his frown.

"Now, the basic laser research. Do you have copies of all of it up to this point?"

"Not. .all of it. But we do have more than half."

"Yes, the half that everyone else knows about. Tell me what *else* you have, quickly!"

"We have two men working in the complex where the labs and experimental shops are situated. We have another man in communications and one more in Skysweeper plans and programs. I know what they are doing. I know of all the tests coming up. The basic research is harder to obtain. Already we have lost one man caught smuggling plans out in his lunch box."

"That was the ultimate in stupidity!" Bolan snapped. "The man should have been shot, not fired. We do not pay you to fail, Smith. Even you must understand that."

"But we are watched, checked. Security is tighter than I have ever seen it here."

"Of course. That is why you get paid well for taking the risks. Now, if you are unhappy in your work, we can move one of our alternates up to take your place."

"No! No, it is only a small delay. We have a new source for the basic research material. We should have it in a week."

"Microfilmed and ready to send?"

"Yes, all ready."

The Executioner seemed to weigh the matter. "All right, one more week. You must be absolutely certain to arrange a failure on the next series of tests. It would move them back months. I trust you have it set up as instructed? Now, show me your safe. I want to see exactly what you have ready for shipment and how much cash you have for emergencies.''

"Yes, of course.'' Smith hesitated. "My usual contact has never asked to see the safe. I was told never to show it, especially to someone who hasn't presented any ID.''

"Smith, you idiot! Do you think we have anything written down? That we would carry any type of identification? Perhaps that is why I have had to replace your contact. You will get a new contact tomorrow. Now, quickly, the safe.''

By the time they had moved to a back bedroom, Bolan knew exactly where Smith carried his weapon. Smith had touched it twice to loosen it in the holster. He twirled the dial of the safe, and when it unlocked he swung on Bolan and Dr. Peterson with a drawn .38 revolver.

The Executioner slammed his fist down on the back of Smith's gun hand, cracking the small bones. The man dropped the weapon and clutched his shattered hand, his face contorted in agony.

"You broke my hand!'' he screeched.
Bolan frisked the man and found a hideout derringer in a boot holster under his pant leg.

"You're not my shadow agent,'' the guy gasped. "Who the hell are you?''

"I'll ask the questions. Open the safe and place everything in it on the dresser.'' The man did not move, but continued to stare at Bolan. Before Smith knew what was happening, the Executioner hammered a karate chop into his kidney. Smith yowled in pain, his body arching backward, his good hand trying to rub the spot where he received the excruciating blow. Then he stumbled to the safe, pulled it open and began to stack papers and two bundles of cash on the dresser.

"Now, lie facedown on the floor," the Executioner ordered.

Smith scowled and did not move. "I'm calling your bluff, whoever you are."

Bolan triggered the silenced Beretta. The slug slammed into the man's thigh and he hit the ground as if his legs were yanked out from under him. Dr. Peterson took a step backward, his face a curious mixture of anger and delight.

"Goddamn it, you didn't have to shoot me!" Smith bellowed.

Bolan decided to drop the "foreigner" act. "That was your bonus for spying against your country."

"Hell, you can't prove a thing," Smith said, wrapping his shirt around his wounded thigh to stop the bleeding.

"I don't have to. You admitted your guilt."

Ignoring the pain, Smith roared and leaped toward Dr. Peterson, snaking his left hand around he scientist's throat.

"Drop the weapon or I break his neck."

Bolan could see the muscles tense in the man's forearm, and the physicist's face beginning to turn splotchy red.

Bolan let the Beretta fall to the floor. There was no time for a standoff and he didn't want the scientist hurt. There would be a better time to take out the traitor soon.

"Kick it over here to me," Smith said.

To reach the gun Smith would have to give up his death hold. Bolan shook his head.

"Not a chance."

Smith increased the pressure on Dr. Peterson's neck and Bolan saw the veins begin to stand out on his temples.

"Do it, or he dies."

Bolan kicked the gun and it skittered to within four feet of Smith.

Bolan started forward.

Smith was suspicious, expecting something.

"Don't move. I'll get it." Smith prodded the scientist ahead, then tried to reach down, keeping his armlock on his captive. For one heartbeat Smith's gaze left Bolan's face, trying to locate the weapon.

Smith tried to force Peterson downward. The physicist resisted. Finally Smith relaxed his hold and began a dive for the gun.

Incredulous, Dr. Peterson watched as Bolan moved faster than the scientist thought was humanly possible. The Executioner slashed out with his right foot, his heavy boot toe connecting with Smith's chin, snapping his head back. A sickening crack resounded across the room. Smith's head lolled to one side as he fell to the floor. He was dead.

The Executioner swept up the weapon and looked at Dr. Peterson.

"You okay?"

"Yes, a little bruised but alive. Thank you."

Bolan worked quickly. He searched the small

house and found female clothing next to Smith's in the bedroom. There were cosmetics and hair-care items in the bathroom. The Executioner hoped the woman who shared the place didn't come in now. He put the contents of the safe in a paper sack from the kitchen. He found a 9mm Soviet-made Stechin automatic machine pistol in the other bedroom. He muffled it with two pillows and fired it twice into the mattress, then wiped it clean of prints, put it in Smith's hand and curled his stiffening fingers around it.

He gave Dr. Peterson the contents of the safe to carry as they went outside. The Executioner re-trieved the dead sniper from the wooden box in the alley, carried him into the house and dumped him on the living-room floor. Bolan put the man's pistol beside the hand of the corpse.

The Executioner straightened up, looked around the room, then nodded.

It would look convincing enough. Bolan was sweating now. He took the two shot-up pillows and moved quietly to the back door. He had turned off all the lights in the house and now slipped out quiet-ly. Dr. Peterson was close beside him.

Everything appeared safe and peaceful. They ran along a block wall toward the alley, then-stopped and checked it all again. Bolan sensed something wrong. Someone was out there waiting for them.

About thirty feet ahead down the alley, Bolan saw a shadow move on the left side. He froze and knelt beside the end of the wall. He motioned for

Dr. Peterson to stay down. The specter moved again and the Executioner heard the soft cough of a silenced weapon. The cement beside his shoulder shattered as a slug slammed into it.

2

United States Air Force pilot First Lieutenant Roth Ludlow had done everything "smart" to stay out of the fighting in Vietnam. He had been in college at the time of the draft. At once he signed up for Air ROTC. He kept his grades up, reported to his draft board, followed the rules and procedures to the letter. When he graduated from college with a bachelor's degree in physics, the Air Force said they would not activate any reserve commissioned nonpilots from the ROTC graduates.

Within two weeks the air war had changed in Vietnam as the Air Force began losing more and more planes and pilots. The word went out that all Air ROTC newly commissioned officers had their choice; they could be activated at once and apply for the duty of their choice, including flight training. Or they could wait and be activated and take any assignment they were given.

Again Roth Ludlow chose the smart way and signed up the next week for flight training. He was not a gung ho militant. Rather he had evaluated his chances, looked over the alternatives and decided that flight training was the best route for him.

A year later he was in the middle of some of the toughest ground-support work the Air Force had ever done.

ROTH LUDLOW WATCHED the green blur of the tropical jungle flash past below him as he thought of today's mission. A company-sized search-and-destroy squadron had fanned out into the dense forest and got pinned down. He and three other F-100 Super Sabre fighters were called in for close support. It was the usual type of operation. The GIs got trapped and now they wanted some friendly fire to keep the Cong busy so they could bug out.

Only in this now-you-see-them-now-you-don't kind of war there were damn few fixed targets. A hundred Viet Cong could make a lightning raid on a U.S. operation, and ten minutes later the entire raiding party could be hiding in networks of underground tunnels, working benignly in the fields or going about other normal civilian routines.

The enemy was harder to find than to kill.

Lately there had been more enemy ground fire aimed at military aircraft. Usually rifle and machine-gun fire from the ground meant little against bomber jets. However even the swift Air Force F-100 sometimes became easy prey on low-level support missions. If five hundred rifles and machine guns fired at one F-100 that was only two hundred feet off the deck, bad things were likely to happen at least part of the time.

Ludlow tried never to think of that. He had

made his bargain. He played his hand the best way he knew how, even after Uncle Sam had rushed in and raised his bet. Now he had to stay in the game any way he could. He would complete his tour and fly his ass out of there for home at the first opportunity.

He slanted off to the right near the yellow smoke coming from a cleared space in the double canopy jungle. The tops of the trees below were more than one hundred feet from the ground. Under them was a secondary layer of thick growth that made any visual penetration to the ground impossible. The yellow plume showed the location of the friendly forces. The Cong were holding a small hill to the left and evidently controlling the advance and retreat of the GIs.

Ludlow checked the brow of the hill, which was not covered by the jungle. He was three hundred yards to the left but drew winking red splotches of ground fire. He zigged to the left and climbed away from the gunners. At least he knew where some of them were.

He led the other three planes to the target, firing a salvo of sixteen rockets from the wing pods. The hilltop exploded with four times that many bright flashes of death as he and the other jets peeled away to the right, climbing for safety into the blue sky. He saw a star blossom on his Plexiglas canopy where a rifle round struck, then he was past the danger zone.

He had spotted heavy ground fire coming from another opening in the canopy on his right and buzzed it, then swung wide when it erupted with a thunderstorm of winking lights. He radioed his flanker pilots that he was taking one run at the spot, then they would make another pass to see if they had provided enough mobile artillery to get the GIs out of there.

Ludlow swung around, gave himself plenty of altitude and held it a hair longer than usual as he lined up on the target, waited a moment, then pressed the firing button. He felt a lurch as the rockets burst from the wing and flew toward the ground fire that was erupting again.

He heard and felt the rounds hit his wings, and he knew the Cong had captured at least one 50-caliber machine gun down there. Another round starred the canopy again, then a dozen more slugs hit his plane as he turned his belly to the fire and jetted up and away.

He noticed the oil-pressure needle dropping to zero. Then the engine sputtered and the roar died as it flamed out. Quickly he checked his list of emergency procedures. Altitude: twenty-five hundred feet. Fuel: forty percent. Plenty, since he wasn't using any. Position: somewhere between Hue and Da Nang.

He tried an air start. Nothing. He tried again. His radio crackled.

"Skipper, you're running dry over there."

"Roger, Skipjack One. Bone dry and no air start. I'm going to take a walk. Mark my spot and call the chopper." He had to bail out. The F-100 glided like a rock, maybe half a foot forward for every foot it fell. No time left. He ticked off the ejection routine, jerked the handle and felt as if somebody had hit him in the back of the neck with a baseball bat as the explosive charges slammed him skyward and away from the doomed Super Sabre.

Then he was out of the plane, the ejection seat falling away, the parachute deploying automatically over his head. He saw three sleek Super Sabres moving in a wide circle around him. He knew they had called for the recovery helicopter.

As he floated down he eyed the terrain below. He was a little to one side of the double canopy area. Thank God for that. He would have to battle through only one leafy mass to get to the ground. He wanted to wipe sweat off his face, but left his helmet on. It would help protect him in the landing.

Ludlow wondered if the rescue bird had taken off yet. If they sent in the Sikorsky HH-3E it could be on site less than fifteen minutes after he hit the ground. He hoped like hell they brought along a Cobra gunship as cover. Damn, he had seen what those babies could do. They had devastating firepower: a 40mm grenade launcher, a Gatling type minigun that could kick out seven thousand rounds per minute and a whole barrage of air-to-ground rockets.

Then he thought of more immediate problems, such as how far was he from all that ground fire? Was he anywhere near those pinned-down GIs? Could he join them? Just how many damn Vietcong were down there in those trees and swamps waiting for him?

His answer came almost at once. A rifle bullet

sang past him and made a small hole in his chute. He jerked the shroud lines as he swung away from the report. Then all he could think of was the trees below. He had never seen so much greenery in his life. Dozens of towering teaks stabbed into the sky with cascades of leaves, shorter evergreen oaks, Japanese cedar and whole forests of bamboo. Then below he could see the familiar shape of hundreds of banana trees.

He unzipped a pocket at his side and pulled out a .45 automatic. At least he had some protection. He wished he had a few extra loaded magazines.

Ludlow's foot hit the top of a tree, but a light breeze carried him over it. Then he crashed through the high branches of another tree. He dangled, still twenty feet off the ground. For a moment he swung there, then caught a branch and pulled himself up three feet to a larger branch. A moment later he had unsnapped his parachute and perched in the crotch of the tree like some kind of skinny white ape.

For a moment he thought he would just stay there in the tree. The Cong would never find him up there. But at once he realized his chute was a big white arrow pointing out his landing place. Also, the rescue chopper would never find him in this foliage. He keyed the radio device in his pocket, which sent out a signal to the bird, then began working carefully down the tree. He didn't want to fall and get a broken leg now. The chopper should be here in ten minutes. Before then he had to find a clearing where the bird could land.

He needed both his hands to climb, so he put the .45 in his pocket.

Three shots blasted through the green silence the moment he stepped to the ground. A trio of Vietcong in tattered uniforms jumped from behind trees where they had been hiding as they waited for him. He had no chance to go for the .45.

A half hour later seven more Cong surrounded him. He was stripped naked, tied with a rope around his neck and hands bound behind his back. A thin wire strand was fastened to his scrotum. He walked with six soldiers in front and four behind. Whenever he didn't move fast enough or failed to respond to the head man's broken-English order, his captors pulled on the wire that ensnared his genitals. Once he fell on his face in the mulch. The pain was excruciating, and the agony became so debilitating he could barely walk.

Many times Ludlow heard aircraft overhead, and once the unmistakable throb of a Cobra gunship. Whenever the planes were near, the procession crouched under the forty-foot-high canopy and waited for them to leave.

As the pilot shuffled forward, one of the men pushed a stick between his ankles, tripping him. They all laughed. A small man with no teeth came up to Ludlow, bowed and then slammed a bamboo cane across his bare buttocks. The others joined in the fun until Ludlow kept falling with each blow. After a few minutes their leader made them stop.

Five grueling miles later, they entered a village. Ludlow was shoved inside a bamboo cage three feet square and three feet high. He could sit down but had to fold his legs. They snipped the wire from his testicles and unfastened the rope from his neck. But his hands were left tied behind him.

He yelped as someone jabbed him in the back with a sharpened stick. When he turned another hit him in the side. A woman laughed and jabbed again. A dozen children, all with sharp sticks, ran up and poked at him. Most of the thrusts broke the skin and he bled.

A half hour later he had puncture wounds over most of his body. The man with some English came out of a hut and stared savagely at Ludlow.

The VC spat in the pilot's face. "Your jet kill my brother today. In three more days you wish you not ever born!"

3

Bolan and Dr. Peterson crouched beside the wall near the Smith house in Ridgecrest. Bolan tried to figure it. The sniper who had shot at them from the shadows ahead must have seen them come out of the house and knew they did not belong there. The Executioner watched the shadow. It did not move.

"*Astanofka!*" Bolan said in a stage whisper the Russian word for "stop."

There was a pause, a chuckle, and two more silenced shots ricocheted off the wall just over Bolan's head. He decided to try another tack.

"What the hell are you trying to do?" Bolan called just loud enough for the other man to hear but not attract any unwanted attention.

"You two don't belong here."

The voice was educated, a native American accent and just polished enough to cause the Executioner some problems. Obviously this was not any backyard hoodlum.

"You know all Smith's contacts?"

"No."

"Then you better make yourself scarce before you find yourself in real trouble."

There was silence. The man was smart enough

to consider the possibility. Some hired go-between perhaps, not a KGB operative. Small fry.

"I got orders. And you are not part of them."

The man in the shadows fired again, but the shot was wide this time. Bolan triggered two rounds from the Beretta, bracketing the sound, punching into the dark shadow. He heard a yelp and then a growl. Two more shots blazed at the Executioner and Dr. Peterson. Bolan returned fire, lower this time. He heard a groan.

"Let's move out," Bolan said to his companion. "He must be out of ammo by now." He left the pillows, Dr. Peterson picked up the sack and they ran down the alley the other way. But no more responses came from the dark shadow behind them.

In the blackness Bruce Martin gritted his teeth as he wound a handkerchief around the bullet crease on his right arm. Nothing serious, but it made him drop his weapon, which was now empty anyway, and let the burglars get away. The other rounds had missed him, slanted off the heavy plank. But now he had to get inside fast and see if Smith was all right and if anything valuable had been stolen. He made sure the men had left, then Martin sprinted to the back door of the Smith house, edged it open and stepped inside.

He snapped the lights on and saw the body at once. Then he looked where he knew the safe was, and found Smith's silent form and the safe still open and empty. Martin checked the corpses for pulses. Nothing, both dead. He picked up the telephone and dialed a local number. Quickly, and using a simple group of code words, he described the situation and received his instructions.

It took Martin nearly a half hour to load the two bodies into his car, cover them with a blanket and drive to the point in the desert he had used before. When he had them both buried deep, he piled the biggest rocks he could find on top of the sand so it would not blow away or wash out. He drove back to town and phoned the number again, reporting the bodies were gone, all signs of violence removed from the house, the safe shut and the house closed and locked.

"Good work, Martin," the voice said. "There will be a new contact for you shortly. Tell me what you can about the men who killed our people."

Martin could not give him much. "One was tall, over six feet I'd say. His voice was deep. He knew some Russian. And he talked as if he was sure of himself, like he was in charge. The other one didn't speak."

"Nothing more?"

"No, it was dark as hell in that alley."

"Okay, Martin. You will receive a bonus. Now go to work as usual tomorrow. But do not go near the Smith house. He has simply disappeared. His neighbors will notice and report it."

"Yes, sir, I understand."

JOSEPH VISHNEVETSKY cradled the phone and rubbed his chin. Yes, he would see that Martin was well rewarded. Quickly Vishnevetsky dismissed the thought and contemplated this new development. This was no simple burglary. The attackers had taken out Luiz in the alley before they went inside. They knew there was a safe and had the contents. But was it the CIA or the FBI? Somehow he thought the killers were neither one. Besides, CIA only operated offshore.

Vishnevetsky sat at his desk and touched his fingers together, tapping them thoughtfully. Base security? Military police? None of them seemed right. All of them might kill one man, but they would keep one alive at all costs to interrogate. Unusual.

Vishnevetsky did not look like a top-ranked KGB field operative, but he was. He was short, balding, with a round face and rosy pink cheeks. Most people in Ridgecrest who knew him thought of him as the short fat man who told more jokes than they wanted to listen to.

Now his smile was gone. He was not in his small used-book store on Main Street. He was considering a serious breach in his operation. Smith had been his main project operative, his lead man with six other Americans gathering information, getting actual copies of top secret plans, learning everything they could about "Operation Skysweeper." They must obtain the complete detailed plans on the project before it ended in two weeks.

Luiz could be replaced and so could Smith, but it would take more time. And he would have to reveal himself to another American. He preferred to sit in the background and let his puppets pull the strings. Money was no problem. Any loss of cash from the Smith safe was insignificant.

As Vishnevetsky sipped at the tall glass of vodka and orange juice, he thought of the replacement problem. Of the four persons left who had been helping Smith, only one had real potential.

Yes, Kara would be a good lieutenant for the close of the operation here. And with success, he would abandon the bookstore and move on. But first, Operation Skysweeper.

Vishnevetsky reached for the phone. He would contact Kara now, give her the good news, and five thousand dollars to do with as she pleased. She might be happy enough to stay the night. She had once before. Yes, he smiled broadly now. Kara would work out well, in two or three areas.

Vishnevetsky took another sip of his drink as he reflected on his career. He had come up "late" in the KGB. He was one of the new breed of agents, had attended the best schools, been moved ahead into the prestigious Institute for International Studies, where he completed intensive courses in foreign cultures and languages. He had the right family connections, he was bright and dedicated.

After graduation he received a minor attaché posting to a Mideast country for three years. When that stint was completed he was called back to Moscow, where he was installed in a four-room apartment, spacious and luxurious by Russian standards. He could buy any Western item he wanted at giveaway prices at a special store reserved for party elite only. Naturally his friends were other special people heading for the KGB. He married the prettiest of the group, whose father was a high functionary in the KGB. A father-in-law like Vasili Gusev could never hurt anyone's career.

Vishnevetsky sipped the drink, remembering. Four children and four promotions. His father-in-law loved his only daughter and worshiped his four grandchildren. One more major coup and Vishnevetsky could write his own assignment back in Moscow. He had ten years in the field, longer than average.

All he had to do was take home the detailed plans for the new laser antimissile weapon, Skysweeper. The plans and copies of the research and all the test data he could get. He hated to admit it, but somehow the Americans had broken through and solved several of the laser-beam technical problems. Skysweeper was twenty years ahead of the Russian scientists.

Skysweeper would be the crowning achievement of his field career. Then he would move into management, desk work, perhaps someday he could be director-general of the KGB! It was heady stuff. But first Skysweeper. And these men who had violated his territory. He must find out who they were and eliminate them as quickly as possible. That was his second order of business.

Kara. He would invite her over for a conference, with just a hint at a promotion on the phone. Then when he told her, she would be more than ready to show her appreciation to Mother

Russia and to him on a more personal basis. He checked the time: too late tonight. Tomorrow for sure. Then he would worry about the men who killed Smith.

4

In their dash down the alley after wounding the ambusher, Mack Bolan and Dr. Peterson got away clean. Bolan figured the gunman would go into the house at once. The Executioner's guess was that before morning the man who had fired at them would make sure all signs of death and illegal entry were removed. The KGB people had a way of cleaning up after themselves. They didn't like murder investigations concerning their helpers. Even now the corpses of Smith and the gunman were probably enjoying a common grave out in the desert.

Making sure they weren't being tailed, the Executioner led Dr. Peterson on a quick walk two blocks to his car. Then they drove a mile and a half to the scientist's house on the other side of town. The physicist had been silent on the way home. Twice he had started to say something, but each time he stopped. Bolan had observed the worried look on Dr. Peterson's face. Perhaps the gravity of this highly dangerous game was only now beginning to sink in.

Bolan had found Dr. Peterson's name on a list that was part of those KGB files Bolan had obtained on his mission to Russia. It was his one source for tracking down KGB operatives and projects in the United States and around the world.

That was his current pursuit, the terror machine of the KGB. In his former role as Colonel John Phoenix, he had operated under official U.S. sanction. But now he was on his own again, freed from the constraints of government bureaucracy. Only occasionally did he receive help from his erstwhile allies.

This way he operated exactly where he wanted to, where the enemy dictated that he must fight to defeat them.

Yes, he functioned outside the law quite often, but with high regard for law-enforcement officers. And he would go to great lengths to avoid any confrontation with the police.

In his personal journal Bolan once wrote: "I'm not above the law. In the final analysis, justice under law is the only hope for mankind. But sometimes a man just can't go by the book. I can't turn away from a fight simply because it conflicts with certain principles. There is a higher ideal at work here. At the same time, I have to keep my respect for the law. We are working toward the same end."

Bolan had known from the start that the world was a frightening jungle, where the first law always had been survival. Perhaps Bolan's decision to travel alone once more came from this basic jungle law. He was an excellent fighter in every aspect. And this came from years of living on the edge, honing his survival instinct.

Bolan often wondered how much difference one man could make. Years of experience had taught him how much a single individual could accomplish—if that person had a total commitment to his ideals. But he had to harden his resolve, and be willing to wade knee-deep in enemy blood to achieve his goal. All he required was the necessary tools, the determination and dedication, never losing sight of his objective, and he could walk that extra mile.

Mack Bolan was the man who could do it. He had proved it before, and here in the blistering desert he would prove it again. But few would know. He did not battle the KGB for glory. He wanted no headlines, no medals.

Only justice.

He wanted some touch of humanity left in the world where innocents were free to wander without threat.

Bolan had started on this mission two days ago. He'd explained carefully to Dr. Peterson the risks involved. When Dr. Peterson said he knew where his contact lived, the man who would funnel secret material to the Russians, Bolan had planned with him to visit the safe house.

Now Bolan sat at the kitchen table as Dr. Peterson prepared instant coffee. The scientist had just seen two men killed. He was badly shaken and Bolan had to get him squared away if he was going to be any more help on this project.

The coffee came, they stirred and sipped. Bolan stared over his cup at the scientist.

"I killed two men tonight. Does that bother you?"

"No. At my age, I have come to terms with violence although I'm a peace-loving man. But it shames me that I have been so weak and helped the Russians. That I caved in after only one meeting with Smith, who threatened my parents. The mere hint of danger to them was all I needed.

"Then tonight I saw what these men are truly capable of. They do not simply threaten, they kill and maim. And I had been helping them, but no more. I am glad that I've found someone like you to help me."

"Good. I'll need your help to get inside the research base."

"That won't be a problem. I am the number-two man on this project. We have been given almost carte blanche to get it completed successfully. My signature is almost as good around the Naval Weapons Center as the President's. I'm not bragging when I say I can get you into any section of the base."

Bolan felt a burden lift from his shoulders. He held out his hand to the scientist. The man grabbed it and pumped it enthusiastically.

"I'll set you up with badges and clearance for anything on base first thing in the morning."

Peterson took a pull on his coffee and stared at Bolan.

"I promised myself not to ask who you really are or who you work with, but I am curious. Guess it doesn't matter a whit, as long as we get the job done, right?"

"Right."

Bolan opened the paper sack filled with the

things from the Smith safe. He spilled the contents onto the table.

"Recognize any of the items?"

Dr. Peterson picked up the document marked Top Secret and frowned. "I didn't think he had stolen this yet. It doesn't matter, that whole basic design has been changed."

Bolan riffled through the pages and found data about laser technology that was so advanced, he could not even recognize most of the words.

"Look at this," Dr. Peterson said. "A list of six phone numbers. I wonder what they have to do with Smith's operation. At least my number isn't there."

Bolan picked up the two packets of U.S. bank notes and passed one to the scientist. "Count this for me, would you?"

By the time they finished they found the tally to be slightly over $30,000. Then Bolan looked up at Peterson.

"Do you know who Smith reported to?"

"No, he never said. I thought he had some contact at an embassy somewhere."

"I'll find out." Bolan shuffled the papers. "Which of these should we destroy?"

"They are only copies. All of them should be shredded or burned. We could use the fireplace right now."

They tore the documents into strips and fed them into the hearth.

Bolan finished his coffee and drew up a chair. "Now, Dr. Peterson, tell me everything we haven't already covered about Skysweeper."

Peterson nodded. "Generally the research is

done. It has been for almost a year. Dr. Roth Ludlow made the breakthrough and is now the director of the project to get it into practical form and then into production.

"It is unlike anything we have had before. With ten or fifteen of these lasers surrounding the United States in parking orbits at twenty-two thousand miles, we could sweep the sky of every single enemy missile that Russia could aim at us. There is no running-dry problem, no ten percent of the enemy missiles that would get through. It is an amazing weapon and one that could insure world peace for the next hundred years.

"Conservatively, we are twenty years ahead of the Russians on this one. That is why they are trying so hard to get the research secrets and destroy our test projects. They have stopped only one of twenty-two tests we have conducted."

"What about this Dr. Ludlow?" Bolan asked. "Can we trust him?"

"He's the only reason I came up here from UCLA to work on the program. Roth Ludlow is a near genius. He is dedicated, a brilliant 'what if' man and a good friend. I'd say right now he's the most valuable single individual in the entire United States defense establishment. He was an Air Force pilot in Vietnam.

"He is not an easy man to know. Tends to be a bit moody and something of a loner. He has a beautiful and gracious wife, and two kids. But there is no way Smith or his people could subvert him, blackmail him, even get close to him. So they have to work through others."

"So Dr. Ludlow is not one of our problems? He would not sell out?"

"I'd stake my life on that, Mack."

Bolan had told Dr. Peterson his name was Mack Scott, a cover name he had used before. The scientist sighed wearily as he looked at the Executioner.

"I should get a couple of hours sleep if I want to function tomorrow," Dr. Peterson said.

He noticed the puzzled expression on Bolan's face.

"Mack, the one guy in the whole place you don't have to worry about is Roth Ludlow. There is not a chance in the world that he could be involved."

5

First Lieutenant Roth Ludlow, USAF, sat in his small cell-like room in a special "rehabilitation and retraining" center just south of Hanoi. Life had been much better lately. For a while there, just after his capture, he had considered suicide. There was nothing to look forward to but pain, torture, degradation and continual verbal and physical attacks. He came close to taking his life one night in the dark when he was trying to sleep a foot away from his own excrement.

The first month had been the worst. He had been moved from one village to another in the tiger cage. He had become a perpetual naked curiosity and a manifestation of the American enemy, who were fighting the VC and bombing them. They vented their rage on him. They jabbed him, spit on him, and the old men delighted in urinating on him.

At last he was transferred to a prison compound where he was confined to a large barracks-type room, given clothes and then interrogated for twenty-four hours straight. But he did not break. He told them his name, rank and serial number, and then began inventing all sorts of fanciful stories. By the time they found out each one was not true, days had elapsed.

His nose had been broken twice, his arm twisted behind him until it nearly broke, and one knee dislocated. He had told a friend in the compound how to pop it back into place, and a week later the leg was back to normal. A smash on the skull with a teakwood club had left him partially blind in one eye for a week, but that gradually improved.

He had been in the camp four months when he and four other prisoners were hauled out of the compound, told to take showers and cut their hair, then were given new clothes and shoes. He had not seen a pair of shoes since his flight boots had been taken from him the day of his capture.

When they talked in the shower they discovered all five were officers, four pilots and an infantry captain. They were put on a truck and taken into Hanoi where they were interviewed separately. Ludlow never saw the others again. The talk was conducted by a Vietnamese officer who spoke English like an American.

He offered Ludlow cigarettes, a candy bar and a bottle of Coca-Cola. In an hour and a half of tape-recorded conversations, the pilot gave out nothing of military significance but felt almost human again. He enjoyed it while he could, knowing he would be back in the mudhole of a prison camp within hours.

He was not. Instead he was taken to a high-security area, which had individual rooms for each prisoner. There was no rule against talking, and he talked for an hour at his cell door with the prisoners already there. They knew little. But they agreed that living conditions were better than before. They came from various prison camps. None of them knew why he had been brought there.

The next day it began. He had heard of psychological torture. "Brainwashing," some called it. It began with total darkness, thirty-six hours of blackness and noise so he couldn't sleep. Then the questions came, and the instructions. He quickly found that he had a low pain threshold.

Within ten days he learned how weak he was. He would do anything, say anything to gain favor and to get sleep, food and quiet. The part he hated most was when they placed the metal bucket on his head. His hands were tied behind him and they pounded on the pail with a metal rod until he succumbed, screaming.

One day they gave him a revolver and showed him that all six chambers were empty. Then they put one round in, closed the weapon and told him to spin the cylinder. He refused. They knocked him down. After a ten-minute beating he spun the cylinder, aimed the revolver at his foot and pulled the trigger.

Click.

They did it four more times, forcing him to aim the gun at his head. The last time it discharged and for a millisecond he thought he was dead. But his Vietnamese tormentors howled in laughter. They had put a blank in and he only received a third-degree burn on the side of his head.

The next day he met Moskalenko for the first time. He was a full colonel in the Russian army and Ludlow guessed he was in the secret police, too. What did the Russians call them now, the MKVD, or was it the KGB?

For two months Moskalenko visited Ludlow every day. They talked of world power, of peace, of World War II and of America. Moskalenko had spent three years in Washington, D.C., at the Russian embassy.

Colonel Moskalenko was a master psychologist and a talented hypnotist. His subjects never realized they had been hypnotized, so could fear nothing from the sessions. Slowly he had put together a complete file on Ludlow.

At times when Ludlow came back from these sessions he could remember little of their conversation except the good-morning and the handshake. They were a blank, a void, and that worried him. But he was being treated humanely for the first time in nearly eight months. He was eating good food, well prepared and served on a steel mess tray.

After two months of talks with the colonel, Ludlow was moved to a two-man room in another wing. The prisoner inside with him was a corporal from Pittsburgh. He was constantly suspicious, foul-mouthed and angry. His one purpose in life was to kill his jailers and get to the arms-storage room where he could get enough weapons and escape.

Ludlow respected the man for his courage but thought his reasoning was faulty. There wasn't a chance of breaking out of there. Their captors had warned them about that, shown them the security. It was tight.

One day Ludlow went as usual to the sunlit room where a bowl of fruit sat on the table. A cold bottle of Coca-Cola stood beside the fruit.

"Help yourself, Captain. I have promoted you. We hear on the radio all pilots captured will be automatically promoted on their eligibility date, so I have made you a captain. Congratulations."

The colonel wore thick glasses, and as he often did, he shook his head from side to side as he stared at Ludlow.

"No, Captain, you do not need to thank me, you deserve it. You deserve it, Captain Ludlow."

As the Russian officer said his name, Roth Ludlow's head dropped forward. The colonel continued.

"That is correct, Ludlow. You are sleeping. When I say your first name, you will be alert, bright, cheerful, and you will remember none of this interview. Now, good morning, Roth."

Roth Ludlow opened his eyes and looked up.

"Morning, Colonel. Damn fine day out. May I have that Coke? It sure looks good."

"Of course, Roth, that is why I brought it. You have been doing well in your training, Roth. Now I have a special mission for you. It is hard, but you can do it. It is hard because one of your countrymen has been collaborating with the enemy, and he must be eliminated. No, I cannot do it. We need someone inside, someone who knows the man, so he will not suspect. We want you to do the job, Roth Ludlow."

"Collaborating?" Roth asked, suddenly serious. "That is a serious crime, punishable by death by the Uniform Code of Military Justice!"

"True, Roth. True. And the man has been tried in your own court by his peers. He has been condemned and now the execution is waiting. The prisoner committee has asked me to have you do the job, since you are the senior commander here.''

"Yes, sir."

"Do you have any qualms about it?"

"No, sir. An order is an order. I'm a soldier. He is a traitor, and my men have given me the honor of the execution."

"Good, good. I could not have said it better. You will take care of this small task the moment you get back to your cell." The colonel handed Ludlow a thin-bladed, six-inch knife. "You can conceal this from the guards?"

Ludlow smiled. "Of course. These Cong guards are stupid. You know that, sir."

"Yes, but they do give us an excellent laboratory to conduct our experiments, is this not true? You will remember nothing of this. You will begin stalking your victim when the guard brings your evening meal. The guard will say 'food' in English. Then you strike. Afterward you will be taken back to your regular cell and there I will use the words, 'well done' to bring you out of your trance. Do you understand all of this? If you do, repeat it to me verbatim."

Ludlow did, a slight frown on his face.

A few moments later Colonel Moskalenko smiled and used the word he always did to bring Ludlow back from his hypnotic trance. "Baseball," the colonel said.

Roth Ludlow blinked, looked at the partly full bottle of Coke in his hand and took a swig.

"My, but that's good! You don't know how I miss the little things, Colonel."

"Like the Yankees. I saw in the *New York Times* that they lost again yesterday. That puts them well out of the pennant race this year. You are a Yankee fan, are you not, Roth?"

"No, sir, Dodgers."

When the Coke was finished, the colonel told Ludlow to take some of the fruit, indicating that the session was over. Colonel Moskalenko watched Ludlow feel in his pocket and recognize the shape of the knife, but Ludlow didn't say a word. He took the two bananas and went with his guard back to the two-man cell.

That afternoon at four-thirty, Ludlow slit the throat of a corporal in the United States Army, and watched him die. Then the lieutenant was taken to his regular cell, where he and an English-speaking guard talked about baseball for a few minutes.

Roth shook his head. Now he was back in his one-man room. He didn't mind, really. That corporal was starting to get on his nerves. At least the little man had spunk. He was the kind of man who would weather POW camp and come out of it.

Roth was still uncertain what the colonel was trying to do. Talk, that's all they ever did. At first he thought the colonel was trying to set him up to steal an Air Force F-100 aircraft and fly it to China, or some such far-out scheme. Hell, maybe he was just a Russian doing his job, and he liked to talk about baseball.

The next day there were two bottles of Coke on

the table in front of Colonel Moskalenko. Ludlow and the Russian colonel talked about baseball and the chances of the Dodgers, who were still a game and a half out. Ludlow finished both bottles of cola.

Now Moskalenko smiled as he watched the American fall under the hypnotic spell again. The man was a perfect subject, and he carried out post-hypnotic suggestions to the letter. The murder of the corporal yesterday was the final test. Ludlow had passed with high marks and today had no re-collection of it. Ideal! Now the continuing training would proceed, and the deep-seated, intense post-hypnotic contact plan would be burned into Roth Ludlow's brain so that he would respond to it im-mediately even after twenty, perhaps thirty years.

"Roth Ludlow," Colonel Moskalenko began. "You will listen to me carefully and store this in-formation away in your mind. Now listen: Roth Ludlow, you are needed. Roth Ludlow, you are needed. Roth Ludlow, you are needed. Repeat the phrase to me twenty-five times."

The colonel lit a cigar as he listened to the American robot obeying orders. Moskalenko did not count the repetitions. The man would do that automatically and stop when the right number had been reached. Ludlow had been the best student in his group of thirty-five so far. Out of this batch, the whole thing would be worthwhile if one or two of them could become useful later on.

When he had proposed the plan there had been immediate interest, but he had suggested they use tourists, visiting scientists, writers, educators. His superiors decided that would be too risky and would take too much time. However, with some cooperation with their Vietnamese friends where time was not a factor and permission was not needed for an interview, the results could be much better.

The colonel nodded as Ludlow finished.

"Good, good. Now repeat after me each sentence as I give it: I will be ready when I am needed. I will live a normal life, progress in my profession, but whenever I receive a call and the key words, 'baseball needs Roth Ludlow,' are spoken, I will do exactly as ordered."

The prisoner went over the sentences, saying each one out loud two hundred times. He had not faltered, blinked or made any signs of discomfort. It was enough for today. Another month and the intensive post-hypnotic suggestion program would be finished.

When he went back to his cell-like room, Ludlow found a two-week-old copy of the *New York Times*. He cried out in surprise and glee and grabbed it. He read every word on the sports page.

Then the pilot folded the sports section, carefully inserted it in its proper place in the complete newspaper and laid it on his bunk. He blinked back a sudden rush of tears. How he wanted to get out of this place! Some days he thought he would sell his soul to the devil, or to the Viet Cong, just to get back to Da Nang. Soon, dammit! He had to get out of there soon or go crazy!

A month later, Colonel Moskalenko decided that three of his charges were ready. He told them individually that they were being transferred to POW camps near the combat zones, where they would be used to help orient new prisoners who had been captured. He told them three had been selected for their intelligence, their ability to communicate well with other men and their stability under trying conditions. None of the three believed what he said, but a change, any change at that point, was good news.

Ludlow was anxious to go. A new camp meant different security. And if he was closer to the fighting, he would be closer to the American lines.

Colonel Moskalenko had given them a briefing on the war, how the North Vietnamese were winning, how they had captured several large towns and had pushed well beyond the old demilitarized zone just above Quang Tri. He said security would be tight, but as a "pacification officer" Ludlow would have certain privileges in the POW camp.

The three officers met for the first time on the morning they left. All wore crisp green uniforms with their rank on the collar. Ludlow was surprised to see captain's bars on his. Each had a kit bag with more basic necessities than they had seen in months: soap, razor, some dry rations, towel, water purification pills and a complete change of clothes. Then they were given Vietnamese boots that almost fit.

They traveled in a guarded truck for two days. They whispered about escaping but decided to wait until they were as far south as possible. They saw wounded being taken north, and a short time later had to abandon the truck as an air strike hit the trail. All three Americans cheered the Navy F-4 Phantom jet as it roared overhead on a strafing run. The truck was damaged but still ran.

Three miles farther down the trail in dense jungle, they had a flat tire. The three guards and driver worked at changing the tire. As they did so they got into an argument that led to a quick fist-fight, and the three Americans slipped away into the bush, heading due south. They heard shouts and then gunshots behind them. But the four North Vietnamese did not chase them.

A week later the three American officers stumbled on a U.S. search-and-destroy squadron six miles from Hue. The escaped ex-POWs were ill with fever, out of food and had no weapons. They returned with the unsuccessful mission to Hue and were flown at once to Saigon. They were debriefed and four days later they stepped on American soil in San Francisco.

Roth Ludlow knelt down and kissed the black-top at the airport. "I'll never leave the United States of America again!" he said as tears of joy streamed down his face.

6

Bolan was up the next morning before the desert sun cleared the horizon.

He was sitting on a chair in the kitchen, studying a piece of paper, when Dr. Peterson came into the room.

"Got to thinking last night. You never did say, are you with the CIA?"

"You're right, I didn't say." Bolan held up the list of six phone numbers he had taken from Smith's safe. "Recognize any of these numbers?"

Dr. Peterson took the list and scanned it. "The last one is out at NWC, that's short for Naval Weapons Center. I know the exchange code." He stared at the number. "Yep, got it. That's the gym. Some of the older guys had formed a volleyball team and I was the skipper. I used to call to book a court when we wanted to practice."

"Gym. Where is it?"

"Blandy and Dibb Streets, near the commissary."

"Any of the other numbers familiar?"

"No, but they look like they all are in China Lake at the center, or in Ridgecrest."

After breakfast was over, Bolan asked Dr. Peterson for his office number. Next, the Executioner checked the equipment in his rented car. His black aluminum suitcase in the trunk held his weapons. Not the variety he once had; no more Stony Man to shower him with the latest and best in firepower.

Bolan felt more like the old Executioner, when he worked strictly alone. As he checked his weapons, those Pittsfield days so many years ago fired vividly to life.

Bolan was a member of the U.S. Army's Special Forces in Vietnam. He was on his second tour of duty as a sniper specialist when he received word that his parents and his sister were dead and his younger brother, Johnny, was critically wounded.

Bolan was granted emergency leave from the Southeast Asia hellgrounds where he had earned the name The Executioner, to bury his kin. When he returned home he learned that his father, Sam Bolan, had killed Mack's mother and sister. Then the senior Bolan had turned the gun on himself. Only Johnny Bolan had survived the manslaughter-suicide.

The Executioner discovered that the Mafia was the root cause of his family's demise.

As Bolan slammed the trunk lid, it struck him now that those early campaigns when he had confronted the Mob's killer legions head-on were mere blueprints for greater missions to come.

With each successful hit, accomplished in the inimitable Bolan style, he was labeled a killer and a butcher. But on reflection, he suspected that those names were uttered by satisfied, smiling lips. He was hounded by law-enforcement agencies in almost every state and in several foreign countries.

The authorities realized there was only one way to soothe the wounded spirit of this rampaging tiger. A pardon.

Bolan was offered amnesty, to work within the law. He agreed—on condition. Because he wasn't finished yet. Uh-uh. He needed one more week to wrap up his Mafia blitz.

His blazing guns spoke the loudest then, spewing deathfire and hellrain on the Mob's six remaining strongholds.

Then, in a fake accident in New York's Central Park, Mack Bolan ceased to exist. But only in the eyes of the public. He was given covert government sanction, plastic surgery and a new identity: Colonel John Phoenix, retired. And by tacit agreement, almost by definition, he became the head of the Stony Man program, operating out of a farm complex and command center in Virginia's Blue Ridge Mountains.

Lifelong friendships were formed with men like Hal Brognola, the FBI agent who had approached Bolan with the Stony Man idea; Leo Turrin, a Justice Department man whom Bolan had met during his Mafia campaigns; Aaron Kurtzman, computer expert extraordinaire; Andrzej Konzaki, ace weaponsmith; and Jack Grimaldi, Mob pilot who decided to change employers when he crossed paths with The Executioner.

Then there was April Rose. If any of the women Bolan had ever met could truly lay claim to his heart, April was the one.

But once more sorrow would shroud the Executioner's existence. During a full-scale assault on Stony Man Farm, April died for the man she loved, cut down by an assassin's bullet.

Bereavement turned to blistering rage as Bolan vowed to seek out the culprit. The Executioner did not have far to go. Bolan smelled treachery as all indicators pointed to a sleeper mole planted in U.S. government circles.

By this time, Bolan was champing at the bit. He felt constrained by the Stony Man aegis. His "sponsors" also discerned a change in the bucking beast and they saddled Bolan with a mission to capture a Russian superhelicopter in Afghanistan.

The Executioner agreed, albeit reluctantly.

In his pursuit of the Dragonfire he killed its Soviet pilot, who happened to be the only son of Major-General Greb Strakhov, head of the KGB's Thirteenth Section.

Bolan was sent back to Russia again, to chaperon the daughter of a longtime friend at an invitational sports meet. Bolan as baby-sitter? The Executioner smiled at the recollection of Kelly Crawford, but his features became grim when he remembered what had followed.

This time the devil was waiting behind the Iron Curtain.

A brilliant plan was conceived and put into effect to trap the Executioner. The KGB created a Bolan look-alike from a Polish dissident languishing in the Gulag. The double was forced to assassinate a worker-party leader in a Russian satellite nation. United States authorities believed Bolan had sold out to the Soviets.

A liquidation mandate was immediately ordered: terminate Bolan on sight. Every intelligence agency was after the Executioner's head.

Bolan escaped from the Soviet Union, but not before wresting from that battleground a KGB master list of operatives and projects around the world. It was all coming together. Because of that list Bolan found the name of the mole who was instrumental in setting up the attack on Stony Man Farm in which April Rose was killed.

The Executioner returned to the States and in one blood-filled night of horror, leaving complete destruction in his wake, he found the mole and executed him in the Oval Office in front of the U.S. President.

Bolan was now beyond sanction. He was on his own once more, unhampered by any rules except his own, answerable to no one except himself. It was the way he liked it. It was the way it had to be.

Bolan mentally reviewed his weapons as he slipped into the rented car. He had his standbys, still in operating condition: his .44 AutoMag, the Beretta 93-R, the Childers Automatic Battle Shotgun, and a disassembled M-16 automatic rifle. He had the usual assortment of C-4 plastique, detonators, magazines and spare boxes of rounds. But he was short on hand grenades, thermite bombs and white phosphorous grenades. He would have to generate some new arms and explosives soon. Perhaps the U.S. Navy could assist him later on.

Bolan wanted to find a telephone other than

Peterson's to call the numbers from Smith's safe and see what response he got. He stopped at a filling station and used one of three booths. It was hot out already. The desert day would be a scorcher.

He tried the gym number first.

"Gym office, Parnelli."

"Wilbur Masconi work there?"

"Not in the last three years. Parnelli does it all here, sir. What can I do for you?"

"Tell me where Masconi is. He said something about seeing Smith."

There was a hesitation, then the man laughed. "Thousands of Smiths, millions I guess. Sorry, can't help you, sir."

Bolan hung up. He would make it a point to see Parnelli. The next number rang six times and no one answered. The third number was grabbed on the first ring.

"Louis's Pool Room, but we ain't open yet."

"Louis there?"

"Speaking."

"Smith told me to call you."

"I'm listening."

"Something about some outside talent."

"I don't know nothing about that."

"Smith doesn't answer his phone."

"So tell me about it. He was supposed to call me here an hour ago."

"You got another number I could call, higher up?"

"Hell no! I don't even want to know if there is one."

"So what do I do now, keep my advance and go home?"

"Talk to Smith. Sometimes he gets busy."

"Like all night? My phone call was made on schedule at three in the morning. Who is busy that time of night?"

"Night people. Don't call me again." Louis hung up.

Interesting. Louis was on the list.

The next call was answered by a young woman.

"Good morning. This is Naval Weapons Center Security. May I help you?"

"Security? Hell, I was trying to get the Center commander's office."

"Sorry, sir." She found the number for him. Bolan mumbled his thanks and hung up.

Security? Why would Smith have such a number? Did he have someone from the security force on his payroll?

There was no answer at the next number and the last one was Dr. Ludlow's secretary. Bolan said he had a wrong number and hung up. Why Dr. Ludlow's secretary? Was she one of Smith's contacts?

The Executioner got back into his car and drove past the Smith house to see if anything was happening. There were no police cars. He pulled a U-turn down the block and came back. The KGB must have cleaned up the scene. But what about the woman? He had seen a woman's clothes in the bedroom. He had assumed a girl lived there.

As he drove toward the house a young woman ran out and hurried down the street ahead of him.

Bolan sized her up. Pretty, maybe thirty, short brown hair, brown eyes, good figure. She looked back at him and then ran faster. She did not see the two-inch lift of the sidewalk where a tree root had raised it. Her toe caught on it and she sprawled on the cement.

Bolan stopped, walked over to her. He bent to help her to her feet.

"Are you okay?"

She jerked her arm away, then looked up with fear on her face. She nodded.

"Yes, I'm fine. Leave me alone."

"I was only trying to help. I thought maybe you hurt yourself." He turned away.

"Wait." She said it quickly, then looked as if she regretted it. "Do you know Mr. Smith?"

Bolan shook his head. "Sorry. I'm new here, don't know anybody but one man, and his name isn't Smith."

"Then you weren't waiting for me to come out?"

"Why would I be? I don't understand...."

"I really need to get away from here. I... I expect someone will be looking for me. There aren't any buses. Could you... would you give me a lift to the center?"

"Of course." He kept holding her hand as he led her to the car.

Bolan opened the passenger door for her, then got in behind the wheel.

Her chin was forward, her soft brown eyes worried.

"Are you in some kind of trouble?" Bolan asked. "You must know this Mr. Smith you asked me about."

"Yes. I was in Los Angeles with some friends, and when I came in this morning he wasn't there. No note or anything. Then they called from his office. He isn't there either."

"What will you do?"

"I don't know. Sammy had a few weird friends, scary. I guess I should stay at a motel."

"You mean these friends of his are dangerous?"

"One of them always had a gun, stayed outside a lot, said it was his job to protect Sammy. I asked him what that meant and he said he couldn't tell me."

"That does sound strange."

"It's more than that, it's crazy. Sammy would have meetings in the middle of the night sometimes. Once I got up to go to the bathroom and there were three strange men staring at me."

"So you want a lift to the center?"

She pondered that. "No. I guess I better go to work." She nodded. "Yes, drop me off at the next corner. I work over there at Clancy's as a hostess. Come in tonight for a good lobster dinner."

"I might do that." Bolan held out his hand. "My name is Mack Scott."

She smiled for the first time.

"I'm Malia."

"Pretty name. Hawaiian, isn't it?"

"Yes, for Mary." She stared at him for a minute, then seemed to make up her mind. "Yes,

Mack, come by tonight about six, I need to talk to someone.'' She slid out of the car and ran into the restaurant at the triangle where Inyokern Street and China Lake Avenue met.

Bolan watched her go. She had been living with Smith, she should know something about what he was doing, but she gave the impression that she did not. Still, she said she wanted to talk. He would be there at six.

He continued on down the street to the main gate of the Naval Weapons Center. Peterson had told him that much of the business end of the center was open. Anyone could drive in. Getting into the restricted area would be harder.

Bolan drove up, told the uniformed Marine guard his name and that he was supposed to pick up his badge and pass at base security. The sentry directed him to the office and said he would notify them Bolan was on his way.

At Security, Bolan produced some ID that he had rigged for Mack Scott of Pasadena. He sat for his picture and soon had his badge marked for top-secret clearance. He pinned it on his jacket, put the ID card in his wallet, then returned to his car.

First the Executioner wanted to check out the gym. It might lead nowhere, but he had to see.

He looked at the information folder the guard had given him. The Naval Weapons Center covered about eighteen hundred square miles. More than five thousand civilians were employed there and some eight hundred military personnel. There was also a fully equipped military airfield, capable of accommodating any Navy or Air Force plane. And there was a variety of ranges: for aircraft and ground work, propulsion facilities and gunnery, combat and test. But the base had as its main function, research and development of new Navy weapons.

Bolan stared at the all-too-familiar characteristics of a military base and frowned. This was going to be harder than it had first looked.

7

Dr. Roth Ludlow sat in his office at the China Lake Naval Weapons Center and tried to relax. He had been tense all morning and he did not know why. Nothing was unusual. Work on the Skysweeper project was continuing on course. They were well into the testing phase and the results looked good so far, just as he had predicted. After all, this was his brainchild, his own private development. He had started the whole thing with a few logical progressions more than three years ago. Then he had spent two years proving his theory. He felt satisfied about the progress on Skysweeper.

Ludlow thought about his family. There were no problems that he was aware of. His son would be starting the sixth grade this fall. Already he was a whiz with a computer. Ludlow smiled. He hoped the boy would follow in his father's footsteps.

His ten-year-old daughter was intensely into ballet and was hoping for a part this fall in her school production of *The Nutcracker*.

His wife Beth was steady and true, his rock, especially at those bad times. Such a strong personality. So much intelligence and spunk in such a little package. Yes, everything was fine. He had made some good financial investments, so there were no money problems. He was thirty-seven years old, gainfully employed and had come within one vote of being nominated for a Nobel prize.

Sure, there were a few snarls at the center, but that was to be expected when fifty or sixty intelligent, sensitive human beings who just happened to be top physicists were all working on the same project. But he had learned how to untangle those snarls.

He was good at human relations, which is what he found himself involved in a lot these days in the waning life of the project.

Ludlow opened a small office refrigerator and took out a cold can of Coca-Cola. He pulled the metal ring on the top of the can and gulped down a couple of mouthfuls.

Drinking the Coke made him think of Vietnam. The first Coke that Russian had given him in Hanoi had tasted so good, he had almost become a turncoat right then. Nam. He thought about it as little as possible these days. It was gone, pushed into the background, but never totally out of his consciousness. And he imagined it lurked somewhere deep in his subconscious as well. Hell, he was no damn psychologist. He had to take things as they came. Right now his priority was to get Operation Skysweeper wrapped up and the hardware so damn perfect that it could go immediately into production. The sound distracted him....

Ludlow turned. Where was it coming from? Then he knew! From the fringe of banana trees just on the other side of the cook hut. Could be a whole damn company of Viet Cong hidden in the grass behind the banana grove.

"Down!" he whispered to the two men with him. "Hell, we haven't got this far to be caught and dragged back to Hanoi!"

The three officers' new green uniforms were now dull black with dirt and stains from five days of crawling through the jungle, wading across streams and trying to hide from the damn VC!

Ludlow motioned for them to stay down.

The chatter of automatic rifles from ahead sent chilling sweat along his spine.

"Keep down!" he shouted to the men. "Let's crawl to the left. Get behind those big trees, then we can run." They had just started to move when a thin Viet Cong woman with a Russian AK-47 automatic rifle in her hands stared down at them.

Ludlow surged up, screaming at the enemy. He charged into her, grabbed the rifle, reversed it and slammed the butt against her head. He heard a sickening crunch as bones broke and her head jolted sideways. In the few seconds he saw the terror on her face, the blood pouring from her nose and ear. Then he was on top of her, his boot crushing down on her crotch, his other foot grinding into her chest as he stepped on her. He was still holding the rifle, running as if his very life depended on it, because it did.

The three fugitives headed south, away from the firing, away from the Viet Cong. The trio charged to the top of a low hill that was so rocky it supported little growth. Now they could see around them.

Directly ahead on a narrow trail they spotted a couple of North Vietnamese regulars digging a hole. After a few minutes, Ludlow saw the enemy soldiers covering the excavation with half-inch-thick sharpened bamboo sticks, jamming one end into the earth, leaving the pointed end sticking straight up. Ludlow had heard of them—punji-stick traps. The top would be covered with straw and light brush to conceal the hole, then some un-suspecting victim would walk into it, fall and the punji sticks would spear into his feet, legs, maybe his torso as he fell.

Ludlow shook his head, still holding the rifle. He led his two companions around the trail and they walked on south, hoping to run into some friendly forces.

A five-man patrol came up on them from be-hind, and the North Vietnamese must have thought they were friendly because of the uniform. One man called out and when Ludlow turned, his finger was stroking the automatic rifle's trigger. He killed three of them with the first burst, and the other two before they could raise their weapons.

"Die, you sons of bitches!" Ludlow heard him-self screaming, as he fired the rest of the rounds into the corpses. Sweat lathered his forehead and he was breathing fast. From far away he heard his name being called....

"Roth! Roth Ludlow, snap out of it!"

The command came faintly, then he heard it

again. As he watched, the Vietnamese jungle wavered, the grinning faces of the dead VC soldiers came back strongly, then the image vanished and he blinked.

He was lying on his office floor behind his desk, holding a ruler and staring at the legs of the small couch next to the window. He shook his head and sat up.

Dr. Harry Peterson shook his shoulder again.

"Roth? Are you all right?"

Ludlow nodded. "Goddamn it! Again. How long was I out of it?"

"Maybe ten minutes. I heard your chair tip over and I came barging in, but you were already gone somewhere."

"Nam. Hell, they find out I'm out of my head they'll fire me."

Peterson laughed. "The way I see it the only person who could fire you is the President. Don't worry about that. We talked once about trying to figure out what triggered these mind flashes. What were you thinking about just before it happened this time?"

"Hell, I don't know. I was a little nervous, uptight about something. That's no excuse. DSS. Delayed Stress Syndrome, that's what the shrinks call it. If I wig out that way on some important test I could blow the whole thing."

Peterson shook his head. "I don't think so, Roth. We have every spot covered twice. Backup. You don't even have to be along on the tests, so it's no problem."

"Who else knows?"

"Your secretary Kara, me and two others. They all are loyal and reliable. Don't worry about that. The project is moving along nicely. The two tests are all set for this week, including the coordination with Vandenberg Air Base."

Roth Ludlow had been sitting on the floor, trying to get his mind and his body working together again. Now he got up and sat in his chair. It would take an hour or more to get back to normal. It always did.

"Perhaps you should take it easy for the rest of the day," Dr. Peterson suggested as he closed the door after him. Ludlow shook his head to clear it again. He shivered and knew he should lie down for a while. That always helped. But he was afraid he would go to sleep and miss a phone call or an appointment.

Busy, stay busy. He looked at his desk and saw the note about talking to his son's science class. He would give them the basics on laser technology. The material was in every textbook, but they liked it better coming from him, a famous scientist.

Quickly he made new notes on some three-by-five cards. It had been a long time since he talked to a class. He decided to practice his little speech:

"A laser is a device that converts incident electromagnetic radiation of mixed frequencies to one of more discrete frequencies of highly simplified and coherent radiation. There are several different types of lasers, but we'll only deal with the carbon dioxide kind, which has proved to be the most useful in military applications."

At this point Dr. Ludlow stopped and made a mental note to keep his explanation of lasers fairly simple to avoid any confusion in the students' minds.

"Now the laser travels at the speed of light, so there is no problem with lead time or target distance. A parking orbit for earth satellites is twenty-two-thousand miles above earth. So in a fraction of a second a laser could go from satellite to earth, or from satellite to incoming missiles fired from anywhere on earth.

"Since aiming and distance are not the basic problems, why has it taken us so long to utilize the laser as a weapon? The problems have been size, intensity, and of course the big one, the tendency of the laser beam to disperse over long distances. It starts out like buckshot from a shotgun. Without a tight choke on the shotgun, the buckshot scatters at a predictable rate. The laser beam does the same thing. The idea is to keep that beam within a four-inch radius after it has traveled a thousand miles, rather than have it spread over a hundred-yard radius. With the dispersion, power is lost, and without the power our laser beam can't be called a death ray.

"Power is another continuing problem. We must find some way to increase the power of the laser beam. If the laser is to be in a jet fighter, the power source can't be the size of this school building. If the power source is to be on an orbiting satellite, the source must be small, lightweight, compact and tremendously powerful."

Dr. Ludlow nodded. Yes, that should be enough

of an introduction. Then he would field questions from the kids.

He was feeling better. He looked at the drawing on the wall. It was an earth view, with twenty-five satellites in parking orbit circling the United States. Each of them contained its own power source and a Ludlow Beam, a killer laser weapon that could fire up to one hundred shots per second from a single platform. They were radar activated, computer controlled and computer fired, each shot locking onto a missile or other selected target. All one hundred shots could be aimed at a single missile, or they could be aimed at one hundred different missiles in the blink of an eye.

He smiled. Once the Ludlow Beam was perfected, the rest of the radar and computer hardware could be ready in a few months. That technology was ready, the satellite know-how was there. All they were waiting for was a practical, working Ludlow Beam that could do the job.

In a secret session, the Senate Armed Forces committee had already approved the mounting and placement of these "killer" satellites. They were waiting for Ludlow's program.

For just a moment a small room in Hanoi flashed before his eyes, and he saw the stern yet kindly face of Colonel Moskalenko, reminding him of something. Ludlow laughed, took a pull on his Coke. He had not thought of the Russian psychologist in years. Strange that he should surface right now. It was probably the mind flash, another association. Ludlow had never been to a psychologist or psychiatrist about his mind flashes. He knew the shrinks would have a field day with him.

He stretched, felt the old energy flowing and looked at his list of Must Do Today items. Quickly he was on the intercom talking to his secretary. It was almost eleven, and he had his whole list to go through yet.

8

Bolan found Dibb Street and turned left to the big gymnasium. The office was just inside the front door. It was so early nothing was stirring yet. Inside the building it was cool, a little more pleasant than the simmering Mojave desert outside. A head popped out from a cubicle as Bolan closed the office door.

"Yes, sir? What can I do for you?"

"Parnelli?"

"Right, sir."

Parnelli was wearing faded blues, apparently not a man to stand on ceremony or uniforms. Bolan pegged him as Navy. The man was stilt thin and sported a short haircut. He looked like a jock.

"What's the setup on volleyball this time of year? Any teams, leagues?"

"No, sir. Volleyball starts in a couple of months. Lots of room in handball and racquetball, though."

"Damn! I'm misfiring again. Sammy Smith said this was the time to sign up."

"Sammy Smith?"

"Yeah. Know him?"

"Know almost everybody at the center."

"That's what Sammy told me. Said you were a good man to know."

"We try. Tell Sammy he still has to sign up, no crashing the schedule." He paused. "You seen Smith this morning? He was supposed to call me."

"Not today. Talked to him yesterday." Bolan stared at the jock. "I don't understand, Parnelli. You have anything for me? A package, an envelope?"

Parnelli frowned. "Man, I don't know what you're talking about. Did I miss something here? I run the gym, that's all."

Bolan grabbed Parnelli's shirtfront and lifted him up on his toes.

"Look, you skinny son of a bitch! I didn't come all the way out to this bake oven just to be jacked around. You get on the phone to Smith and get it straightened out, or Smith's little apparatus is going to be short one man, you!"

Parnelli lost his bravado. He shivered and held up both hands, palms out.

"Okay, okay! Get your hands off me. I'll call. But Sammy never sends nobody without him calling first."

Bolan let go of him and Parnelli picked up the phone. There was no answer.

"Keep trying. Where can I get a drink?"

"This time of day, back in town."

Bolan turned and left a confused Parnelli glaring after him. Parnelli shook his head and dialed the number again, but got no answer.

Half a mile back down Inyokern Street, Bolan

drove out the front gate and found a phone booth. He called one of the numbers that had not answered earlier. Someone picked it up.

"Good morning! What a fine day! This is the Book Rack."

"I'm looking for a book." Bolan gave the name of a popular bestseller.

"Yes, I have it. How many do you need?"

"One will be fine. Where is your store?" Bolan got the address in Ridgecrest and said he would be over shortly. He used the directory in the booth to look up the address for Louis's Pool Room, memorized it and headed down China Lake Boulevard and Highway 178 in the town of Ridgecrest.

Bolan estimated there were about 20,000 residents in the town. The poolroom squatted between two three-story buildings and an Open sign hung in the window. He parked and pushed in through the door. The twin odors of stale beer and sweat hit him along with the blast of air-conditioning. At first he was not sure the lights were on, then he saw a green cloth with a directional shade on a bright light and two men moving around the table.

No one else was in the place. Neither man looked up as Bolan walked over and leaned on the next table, watching the action. The bigger guy with no shirt and a belly flopping over his belt was lining up a shot. The other man was smaller, dressed neatly in a three-piece suit and light blue shirt. Bolan approached the players.

"Louis?" Bolan's parade-ground voice cut across the tension in the room and both men put their cues down and looked up, surprise and a touch of respect in their attitude.

"That's me," the slob said.

"You need to talk to me."

"I need.... Buddy, I'm in the middle of a game." He turned away.

"We talk, *now*!" Bolan said, his voice softer than before, but penetrating.

The well-dressed man held his cue in both hands and came toward the Executioner.

"Sir, I don't think you understand. Louis said he was in a game and as soon as he's finished he'll talk with you."

Bolan grabbed him by both shoulders, lifted him and sat him on the table. Pool balls scattered.

The heavyset player put his cue down and nodded.

"Hell, why not? Sure, I got nothing better to do. In my office?" He looked at the man on the table. "We'll play it again tomorrow, fresh start."

The dapper man got off the table, picked up an expensive attaché case from a covered table and went out the front door.

"This better be good," Louis said.

"Tell me what the hell happened to Smith. He doesn't answer his phone and when I had a man check, his wall safe had been cleaned out. That could be dangerous for your health, Louis."

"Look, mister, I'm not involved. So you have a meeting here now and then, so what? And I don't know who the hell you are."

"Not important. When did you last talk to Smith?"

"Yesterday morning. He called from work."

"Was he worried, nervous?"

"Hell no."

"Then I think somebody's taken him out."

"Who?"

"Maybe you could tell me."

"Me? He liked to shoot pool. We played a game now and then for fifty bucks. No big deal. He had a couple of meetings here with three or four people. I never saw them, came in the back way, left that same way. I don't know what he was into. Drugs?"

Bolan peeled off a fifty-dollar bill from the roll in his pocket and handed it to Louis. "For the pool game I interrupted. Forget I was here, I must have the wrong man. Who was the dude in here when I came?"

"One of the local pushers, coke mostly, now. Nobody to worry about."

Bolan nodded and went out the front door to his car and drove away. He noticed Louis watching him from the window. A normal enough reaction.

The Executioner stopped two blocks down and sat there for a moment, reflecting on the operation. He pulled out the list of telephone numbers he had taken from the safe. He found a phone booth and dialed. Still no answer on the sixth number. He headed for the bookstore.

It was small, sandwiched between a beauty parlor and a supermarket. The place was jammed with books, all used. There was no air-conditioning, just one three-foot fan blowing on the manager, who sat behind a small counter watching a portable TV set. He was short, balding with a few strands of blond hair swept over his bare pate, and had a round face and rosy pink cheeks. He heard Bolan enter and now he looked up and grinned.

"Good morning. Can I help you?"

"I called a while back about a book." Again Bolan gave him the name of the novel.

"Yep, got her right here. Guy tells a pretty good story, but I don't think them Ruskies got anything nearly that advanced in the field of fighters."

"I hear that plane will fly five thousand miles an hour."

"No way the metals we have today can take it."

"Guy I know said it would do more. Mach 5 is three thousand, three hundred and fifty at one hundred thousand altitude. Bet it will do Mach 7. Now that is burning! Oh, this expert says he knows you. Name's Sammy Smith." Bolan watched the book seller closely. Not a blink or twitch, just a casual look upward.

"Smiths I know, but none of them are named Sammy."

Bolan paid for the book, thanked the man and walked out. The Executioner wasn't sure if he had struck a nerve or not. Perhaps the balding little man had been too controlled. Outside, Bolan pretended to study a store window for a moment, checking the bookstore door out of the corner of his eye.

A man wearing a blue tank-top shirt came out fast, saw Bolan and hesitated, then walked the other way.

The Executioner nodded. So he had touched a nerve, and they were going to play tag. Good. It was always fine to know the other players in the game. Bolan strode after the man, who had glanced twice over his shoulder. He stopped and looked in the supermarket, evidently hoping that Bolan would go on by. He did not. Instead Bolan tapped him on the shoulder.

"Pardon me, old boy, would you happen to have a light?" Bolan asked, using a ridiculous English accent.

The man turned, his eyes widened, then he shook his head. Bolan had seen what he wanted to. The man was pure muscle, probably not KGB brand but close enough. When the goon indicated he did not have the light, Bolan shrugged and walked to the corner without looking back. He was sure the thug was behind him. He stopped just around the corner and waited.

Half a minute later, Blue Shirt ran around the building, hit Bolan's outstretched foot and fell to the sidewalk. He did a neat forward roll and came up heading back for Bolan with a six-inch blade in his hand. The Executioner only had time to dodge one way and then pivot. He launched a roundhouse kick with his right foot and felt it thud solidly into the enforcer's stomach muscles.

Then Bolan spun around again, waiting for the man to come at him. Bolan sized up his opponent. He was about six feet tall and Bolan's weight. It could be an interesting contest.

Bolan watched as the knife flicked from one hand to the other.

The man lunged, feinted, twisted and came in again, but Bolan was no longer there.

The man charged again. The Executioner sidestepped neatly, clipping the knifeman behind the ear. He went down in a heap.

Twenty minutes later Bolan pulled his rented Ford to the side of a desert trail and killed the engine. The tank-top goon in the front seat was conscious.

Bolan opened the passenger door and rolled him into the desert sand. They were twenty miles from town, in the middle of some rocky terrain, cacti the only vegetation. The temperature was more than 110 in the shade. The Executioner wiped sweat off his forehead.

"Ready to talk?" Bolan asked the man.

"Yes."

"Who's the guy runs the bookstore?"

"Joe Vishnevotsky."

"Why did he set you onto me?"

"He wanted me to break a few bones, put you in the hospital."

"Why?"

"Don't know why. I just do what he tells me."

"That's what I was afraid of. Did you know he is a Russian spy?"

"Him? He's no damn spy. Runs a bookstore."

"You're dumber than I figured." Bolan cut the cord from the man's feet, then his hands. The Beretta came up, aiming between his eyes. "You like living, hot shot?"

"Sure."

Bolan triggered the 93-R. The slug kicked up sand an inch away from the man's foot.

"You want to do much more of it, you walk out to the road and hitchhike north, away from Ridgecrest. I see you in town again I won't miss. Understand?"

The man frowned, but kept looking at the gun as he nodded.

Bolan slid behind the wheel of the Ford. He wanted to talk to Ludlow's secretary. If he pushed it he could catch her before lunch.

He looked at the muscle standing in the trail behind him. He should be able to find his way out before dark. It would give Vishnevetsky something to think about. Why would a bookstore owner try to have him beaten up? Because he asked a question about Sammy Smith.

Bolan gunned the Ford along the rough road toward the highway. He had a lot of ground to cover before dark.

9

When Bolan called the number at the Naval Weapons Center just after twelve, he was told that Kara Ralston was already at lunch. Bolan decided to grab a bite and kill an hour in a small air-conditioned restaurant. He had a small steak and used the public phone in the lobby to call back at one-thirty.

"Kara Ralston?"

"Speaking."

"Name's Mack Scott. Sammy Smith suggested I give you a call. I'm in town for a few days on business."

He heard a quick intake of breath. But when her voice came on again it was casual, controlled.

"Oh, well, any friend of Sammy's. By the way, have you talked to him today? He was supposed to call me but I haven't heard from him."

"No. Last time we talked was about a week ago. He asked me to meet him but I couldn't get him on the phone today either."

"Could we get together for a drink? I'm off work at four." She asked it casually but there was an undertone of concern. "There's a place called The Hideaway on China Lake Boulevard in Ridgecrest. Could we meet there about four-fifteen?"

"Okay. I'm six-three with black hair and a light tan sport shirt. Sammy said I'd like you."

"Fine, I'll find you. Oh, I'm five-five with short blond hair. Look forward to meeting you. I've got to go now. Bye."

Bolan hung up and looked at his phone list. He still had not had a response from one number. He tried it again and still got no reply. He hung up and called the operator. When Bolan began talking it was fast and with a deadly urgency.

"Operator."

"Operator, this is Sergeant Streib, Ridgecrest police. My partner is in trouble and all I have is a phone number. Get me the address damn quick and no questions! Two men with guns are holding him hostage. I hope I'm not too late." Bolan recited the number to the operator.

"I'm sorry, but it is . . . ."

"Operator! My partner may be dying! I don't want any of your crap about rules and procedures! Just look up the damn address before I come down there and take that office apart!" A drop of sweat dripped off Bolan's nose.

"Yes, all right, officer, I'm checking in our street guide. Here it is. 1444 Windward. That's out on the far edge of town to the west."

Bolan hung up and nodded. The smaller the town, usually the harder it was to get an address that way. He had until four o'clock. He piled into his Ford and drove around the west side of Ridgecrest until he found Windward Street.

He found the house and drove past it slowly. It was a solid-looking, two-story bungalow with a chain link fence all the way around, topped with what looked like insulators on the posts. Electrified? He parked, knocked on the door two houses down and told the woman who answered that he could paint her house for three hundred dollars. She slammed the door in his face. No one was home at the house right beside 1444.

When he knocked on the 1444 door he figured there would be no one there either, but after three knocks a small Mexican woman wearing an apron answered. She looked up at him and smiled, then nodded. She mumbled something, then shook her head.

"No hablo inglés."

"Gracias," Bolan said. He quickly realized he'd be wasting his time trying to get anything from the Hispanic maid. He waved and left. As he walked back to his car he heard two snarling black Dobermans. They were jumping at the chain link fence. The fierce-looking animals were quivering with anger and frustration as they charged the fence. Bolan decided to give this place a wide berth.

The Executioner drove back downtown and parked half a block from the Book Rack, where he had met the man named Vishnevetsky. Bolan mentally reviewed the events so far. Why would the man set his muscle on Bolan unless he had something to hide? He had to be tied in with Smith somehow. What good could a used-book store proprietor do for a known traitor and at least part-time Russian spy? Bolan came up empty. He watched for an hour and nothing happened except for three old ladies who carried in sacks of books.

He drove on and found The Hideaway, which looked like a good steak and seafood eatery. Bolan parked in the lot behind the building and again tried to answer the questions that kept gnawing at him. Smith was some kind of glorified midlevel mule, taking messages and documents back and forth. He was not the ranking KGB man on the site. So who was? None of the people he contacted through those phone numbers seemed to be strong enough to handle the task.

Kara? Not likely. She would need top-secret clearance working for Dr. Ludlow. No way could she have been recruited and trained by the KGB without the security clearance boys getting wind of it. Malia, the Hawaiian woman he was going to have dinner with tonight? Too scared, not the type. She was probably just what she looked like: a working girl taking a free ride and getting room and board for a few romps in the bedroom.

Dr. Peterson? He would not be blowing the whistle on Smith if he was the real Russian agent. That would make no sense.

Bolan got out of the car and walked a mile through the town, came back and entered the restaurant. It was 4:10. Kara should be there soon. She was waiting for him in the bar, first booth on the left. He looked at her and walked over.

"Miss Ralston?"

"Yes. Mr. Scott?"

He nodded and sat down. She was daintily licking the salt around the top of a wide margarita glass.

She smiled. It was a good smile on a thin face,

with narrow arched brows, high cheekbones and wide-set green eyes. Bolan figured she was about thirty.

Bolan ordered a beer and she nodded.

"Still working and not drinking. Does that make you a cop?"

"No. Beer cools me down in this heat. Heard from Smith?"

She looked away, not trying to hide her discomfort. Then her green eyes stared into his. "Not directly. How well did you know him, Mr. Scott?"

"Business, we bumped into each other now and then."

"But you weren't like close friends?"

"No. Met him twice," Bolan admitted.

"Look, I don't want to shock you, but I don't think Mr. Smith is with us anymore. Someone called me and said Sammy had an accident, and it has been taken care of quietly. From all appearances it looks as if he has just vanished."

"Sounds suspicious." His beer came and he took a sip.

Bolan was trying to read the woman and he sensed a nervousness.

"You said you were doing a job for Sammy."

"Right."

"I imagine you knew the details."

"No. We were on a public phone and he said he would fill me in today."

"That is a problem. The person I talked with, one of Sammy's, ah, associates, said he had no idea what kind of a job Sammy might have set up for you."

"The kind of job is easy. I'm a specialist. I brought my equipment. Long range, short range."

She slid closer to him in the booth. Bolan discerned a new kind of awareness in her eyes as she stared at him.

"That's the kind of person who really appeals to me, Mr. Scott." She caught his left hand, moved it under the tabletop and laid it on her thigh. "I hope you understand what I'm talking about, Mr. Scott."

Bolan nodded and grinned. "I do understand. But I always say business first. What the hell happens to my job out here? Am I out of work? Who is taking over for Smith? Damn, I got more questions than I got answers."

Bolan reached over and kissed her lips softly, then sat back.

Her eyes came open slowly. "Hey, I like that. Tell you what I can do. I can find out about this tonight. Did you get any kind of an advance?"

Bolan shook his head. "We trusted each other. Which really leaves me out on a limb."

"I'll find out if there is any work for you. This person will know. If there is, it will be the usual arrangements. If it was something private Smith had going, we can't help you out much. In that case, I'll try to get half your fee as a guarantee."

"Sounds fair."

This time the woman leaned toward Bolan and the kiss was harder, hotter. When she pulled back she sighed and watched him. "I just wish like hell I didn't have this date tonight."

"Tomorrow night? You say where."

"Right here, at four-thirty. We can go for a ride in the desert." She looked at her watch. "Oh, time for me to move." She drained the last of the margarita and pushed out of the booth. She held his chin for a moment, bent over and pecked his lips. "Same place, same time." Then she was gone.

Bolan waited until she was out of the parking lot. He did not want her to think he was trying to follow her—which he damn well wished he could. She had to be seeing Smith's shadow agent tonight. Somewhere in this area, but who and where?

Then he thought of a new problem. He had made himself known to Kara, she would not forget him. If the person she reported to had also met Bolan as Mack Scott in some of his visits today, it could prove more dangerous than ever for him if the two compared notes about him. On that one he would have to wait and see what developed.

He paid for the drinks and left the lounge. Then he got into his Ford and headed for Clancy's Claim Company. The sign said the restaurant featured steak, lobster and spirits as well as entertainment. The talent would not be there yet. Maybe he and Malia could have a quiet little talk.

Malia greeted him as soon as he entered. She was the hostess, as she had said.

"Good evening, sir, the bar or the restaurant?"

"Wherever we can talk the easiest."

She led him to the bar, to a table at the side but not far from her post as hostess. She talked a moment to one of the waitresses and gave her a stack of menus. When she came back Malia was visibly relaxed.

"Someone has been calling me here. Three times now. It's a man and he says Sammy wants to see me. I really don't know what's going on."

Her eyes were somber, not afraid now but not confident either. He decided she was prettier than he had thought this morning. And either scared or giving a good imitation.

"You don't have to worry about Sammy Smith, he's dead. I heard it this afternoon from one of the people in his little spy group." She looked up, surprised. It was enough to tell him a lot.

"So now you can drop the act. We're on the same side. You're undercover, but for whom I don't know yet. Smith was working for some shadow Soviet agent. Smith wasn't smart enough to be a KGB operative, so he had a backup. Our problem is to find out who that backup agent is. Maybe he's the one phoning you. He isn't sure about you, about how much you know. So it might be better if you quit your job, take a week off and go to Los Angeles."

"I don't know what you're talking about. I'm a hostess here and just happen to have been living with Sammy Smith. You come in here with some wild spy story...."

"Give it up, Malia. I read people well. It's time we got out of here."

"Like hell! I don't run when the shooting starts. I've been on this assignment for six months. We knew Smith was the key, but we wanted the man behind him too. I've got ten names and descriptions, but nobody who could be the shadow."

"Lots of time the real agent is the one you would least suspect. Like me."

She looked up quickly and he grinned.

"You're not DIA or I would have pegged you long ago. And you can't be CIA because they don't work domestically."

"How did you tumble to me?"

"Not going all tearful when I told you Smith was dead. You'd been living with him, you should have misted up a little."

"So what good am I around here? Bait?"

"No!" He said it sharply and she glanced up. "I've seen too many pretty girls wind up as turkey meat. No chance you are going to be bait. We'll smoke the shadow out another way."

"Name one."

"When we need one, I'll have one."

"Until then?"

"Smith and his people know you work here, correct?" She nodded. "Well, you just quit. Out the back door, I'll have the car around in a few seconds."

"The kitchen, by the big cooler stacks," she said, moving quickly now, realizing she was in danger, not fully understanding why she was going with this stranger. He made sense, he knew some of the right answers, and he obviously was not one of Smith's men. She told the manager she had to leave and she wasn't sure if she would be back. Then she grabbed her purse and hurried for the kitchen.

As she stepped outside a car roared toward her. She jerked back just in time. It was a blue Chevy and Scott was not driving.

The Ford came around the corner slowly. She heard some small coughs she knew were silenced shots. They came from the Ford, and the man in the blue car folded over the wheel. The car slowed and rolled to a stop near the fence.

The man she knew as Mack Scott drove up to her and she slipped into the vehicle's passenger side. Bolan floored the gas pedal, hustling them ˋway from there.

"Did you know the guy in the blue Chevy?" Bolan asked.

She shook her head. "I've seen him around Smith's house, but no name. He might have been an enforcer, a part-timer I think."

"You ever hear the name Kara Ralston?" Malia shook her head. "What about Joe Vishnevetsky?"

"Yes, he runs a bookstore. Short little man with a bald head."

"He's involved somehow. What about Louis's Pool Room?"

"Sammy used to go down there one or two nights a week, to shoot pool, he told me."

"He never took you along?"

"No."

"Good. You filed all of your data on Smith with Washington?"

"Yes, the usual way."

He took the roll of bills from his pocket. The stack was an inch thick. The rest of the $30,000 was in his weapons suitcase in the Ford's trunk.

"Here's a thousand dollars. It was Smith's mad money. We'll find you a private motel in the area, and we go in under Mr. and Mrs. names. Don't poke your head out of the room or open the door unless it's food, the maid or me."

"I should report in."

"Try it and you'll report in dead."

It took them a half hour to find a motel, and he checked in for both of them under a fake name and drove around to their room. He had requested the second floor and had paid for a week.

They climbed the steps and went into the room. She sat on the bed, then stood up nervously.

Bolan noticed her discomfort.

"You stay here. I'll call you two or three times a day."

"I don't know why I'm trusting you this way. You never did show me any identification."

"Trust me. I think you'll be safe. I've got a house call to make."

"But what . . . ?"

"You've done your part. Now it's my turn to see if we can mop up this little nest of KGB agents and slime before they get out of hand." His voice softened. "Malia, if that's your name, you are one hell of a woman. Now, lock the door after I leave. You'll be hearing from me."

Bolan left the room and heard the lock click behind him. No one was around. Good. He got in the rented Ford and drove back into the center of Ridgecrest. First he'd visit Dr. Peterson, then out to Windward Street. He wanted another look at that high-security safehouse.

10

Bolan made sure no one was following him. He watched for pairs of cars alternating, or any cars that followed him for three blocks or more. There were none.

As he drove toward Dr. Peterson's house he began thinking about this current mission, about the path he had chosen for his life. No, the path, blazed out of hellfire, that had chosen him.

Too often the media's fake tears and agonizing over the criminal dead had been totally one-sided, on the wrong side. In his war against the Mafia, Bolan had opened a lot of eyes to the truth. He had exposed the scum for what they really were— mindless killers.

His antiterrorist wars had been much easier in that respect. There was no good press for terrorists. The world understood, and frighteningly so, their nefarious acts, fired though they were by political idealism.

And now Bolan was on his own again. There was almost no bad press so far, and he was grateful for that. It was one less problem he had to think about.

Sure, he charged into the KGB with his eyes wide open and a raw wound in his heart. Selfish?

Yes, in a tremendously personal way. He was striking back at the bastards who cut down April-Rose. Until his vengeance was sated, he would continue to hound the Soviet terror machine, which was motivated by visions of world domination.

Mack Bolan nodded grimly. He was on the right side, doing what he had to do, and he would carry on the good fight until he died. He hoped when that time came, enough people would have been alerted, and motivated, to take a page from the Executioner's life and follow his example.

Bolan lifted his brows with renewed determination to continue the fight.

He made one more turn, then drove past Dr. Peterson's house and parked down the block, walked back and entered through the side door.

Dr. Peterson was already home. He was excited as he greeted Bolan.

"Good news, Mack. They have moved up our next flight test. We go tomorrow. Somebody said it was to try to make a big publicity splash when the President is here. He's flying in tomorrow morning on Air Force One."

"What kind of a test is it?"

"In-flight. We'll be going after a Sidewinder missile in an air-to-air hit from about two hundred miles. Actually we'll be setting it up for a forty-five-degree, same-altitude shot from the rear—a catch-up, and it will be over the ocean. The area will be swept first with radar for any surface ships or aircraft. None of our other tests have been at this range or this degree of difficulty. A hell of a lot rides on this one.''

"Smith's boys will try to stop you."

"That may be one of the reasons for moving up the schedule. Ludlow is trying to do everything he can to make it work."

"Is it an experiment, or do you know you can make a hit?"

"Shouldn't be any problem, just a longer range to check on our beam-dispersant problem."

"Can you get me aboard the laser plane?"

"Yes. You have clearance with that badge. But why do you want to come along?"

"I've got a gut feeling I should be there. Are all of the men on the test crew checked out by base security for top secret?"

"Ten times over. We even have a continuing check every three months of our twenty key test people—habits, debts, any gambling, spending lots of money, that sort of thing. If there's a ringer in there, I don't know about it. Smith never had me dig into anything about my own people, or ask me to put in one of his people."

"So your personnel checks out. I still want to be along. If the test is going to be sabotaged, it has to be done on the plane."

"True, they would have to have someone in the crew. Hell, I can get you aboard. I have a four-man supernumerary. I can change personnel for any reason, at any time. Of course, I keep them in qualified positions. I can put you in the super-numerary and shift you in at the last minute on a non-tech spot."

"What do you know about Kara Ralston? I think she's involved with the Smith bunch."

"Kara?"

"I talked to her this afternoon. Remember that list of phone numbers I found in the safe. One of them was her private number at the base. She probably screens all incoming calls to Dr. Ludlow. That's why you didn't recognize her own number."

"Good heavens! I better call Roth right now."

"No. Let her stay there for a few days. We mustn't let her be aware of our suspicions. Just be sure anything sensitive doesn't go through her."

"That will be tough."

"You have to do it. Now, how do I get on board that plane tomorrow?"

"Your badge is clearance enough, since I have to approve everyone. We'll simply use the supernumerary gambit and nobody will think a thing about it. I shake up the team this way every so often. No problem. We've got one guy who is about your height, standby radioman. Nothing to do unless the head radio mouth has a heart attack or gets shot. You could watch everyone. I'll tell him just before I post the crew for the test."

"We have to get through the gate."

"You'll ride with me."

"Good. Now, the test tomorrow. Tell me exactly what we do. If there is another plane that fires the Sidewinder, where we'll be, how the whole thing is set up."

Dr. Peterson briefly explained to Bolan the purpose of the shot, roughly how it would be done and what he would need to know.

"I've been working with lasers since early in 1960, and I've helped develop them. The laser can be used in thousands of ways, but the one I'm most interested in is this antimissile work.

"We've got all the components. Now, it's just a matter of putting them all together. Right now we rely on the BMEWS, the Ballistic Missile Early Warning System, of radar stations to give the warning about incoming missiles fired by Russia."

Bolan had never been involved in this end of defense and he listened as the scientist laid out the whole plan.

"The new plan goes around the EWS, utilizing high-powered microwave tracking radar to pick up the first firing of any missiles, lock on to them and give a continuous and rough position of the incoming.

"The tracking radar is supplemented by an optical radar that uses a laser to establish the range down to an inch or so. The optical radar gives the range, elevation and horizontal bearing to a sophisticated computer. All of this equipment is automatic, working through the satellite in parking orbit over the U.S. in a defensive position.

"The computer assigns the best-located laser to fire at the missile at the first opportunity and destroy it in a number of different ways." Then Dr. Peterson got into more complicated aspects of the whole laser picture.

After the scientist finished his explanation, Bolan stood and stretched. He had grasped the fundamentals about what the laser was supposed to do. Tomorrow he would see it in action. He had the test procedure down as much as he could without walking through it. He knew enough about it so nobody could fault him for taking up space in the plane.

"What time is takeoff in the morning?"

"Time of departure from Armitage Field is 0530. I'm going to try to get some sleep. The sharper the better tomorrow."

"When is the President going to arrive?"

"We're not supposed to know but I hear it is about 0700. We're scheduled to shoot about fifteen minutes before then."

"Unless we have a hold." Bolan stood and pushed the silenced Beretta 93-R into his shoulder leather. "I'm going for a ride to view your desert night sky."

"And to do what else?" Peterson asked.

"A house I need to check out on Windward Street. It's tied in somehow. I won't be gone long."

Ten minutes later, Bolan was crouching behind a line of shrubs in the yard of the dark house beside his target. There were no lights on inside the residence behind the chain link fence. He could hear the foot pads of the Doberman guard dogs circling the barrier.

The first test was a soft whistle and then an underhand toss as he threw a half pound of hamburger meat over the fence. A moment later the friendly snarls came as the two dogs shared the unexpected meal. They were not well-trained guard dogs or they would have taken food only from their handler.

Bolan took a quarter-inch-thick steel bar and threw it at the fence. The bar struck the wire, shorted out, and a flash jolted through the darkness. The rod stuck in the fence caused a continuous blue arcing of electricity. Somewhere a bell rang, and at once lights snapped on illuminating the fence and a twenty-foot radius ahead of the Executioner.

The dogs shrank back from the parking fence, licking their chops. For two minutes the lights stayed on, and Bolan guessed the area was covered by hidden video cameras. Somewhere a monitor would show that no human was trying to get inside the compound.

The lights snapped off. Bolan had found out what he wanted: the dogs were for real but could be bribed with hamburger meat, which could be laced with knockout drops; and the fence was highly electrified, probably at night.

He drove back to Peterson's house and called Malia. She picked up the phone on the first ring.

Her voice sounded unusual over the phone.

"Malia?"

"Yes, me, in person in prison. When do I get my parole?"

Bolan ignored Malia's attempt at humor although he understood her plight.

"I'll be gone during the morning tomorrow, but I'll try to stop by later in the day."

"I feel so helpless sitting here, doing nothing. I

was trained to do this work, and here I am cowering in the corner.''

"That's much better than being stuffed in a cardboard box and sent through a garbage grinder.''

"Ugh! Colorful but true. Thanks for reminding me. Isn't there something I can do?''

"Yes, stay out of sight, out of trouble and catch up on your sleep.''

"Yes, sir.'' She paused. "Mack, am I doing the right thing?''

"Yes, you are. You'll probably have to testify if any of these jokers live to stand trial.''

"Oh. I hadn't thought that far. Thanks. Goodnight, Mack.''

"See you tomorrow, Malia.''

THE KC-135 WITH AIR FORCE MARKINGS waited on the runway at the Naval Weapons Center's Armitage airfield when Bolan and Dr. Peterson drove up the next morning. The plane was a workhorse for the Air Force. It served as a flying filling station, as a transport and as a platform for various experiments and tests such as this. The aircraft was designed and developed by Boeing as a prototype for the Air Force, and also for the generation of civilian 707 jet transports that served airlines for fifteen years.

There had been no problem at the gate, and out here Dr. Peterson was in total command. He was the field general, and Dr. Ludlow sat back at the command center tracking the results.

The KC-135 looked little different from others Bolan had seen, with the exception of large Plexiglas panels on each side amidships, just back of the wings. The panels were four feet square and had a strange-looking device that stuck out six inches through the glass. It was a sliding panel that allowed the gun to be moved, only with no exposed open air.

Most of the device was encased in a large rotating cover that looked like stainless steel but was undoubtedly something much stronger.

Dr. Peterson took Bolan to the radio shack and showed him the basic operation. Then the scientist introduced Bolan to the operator when he came, indicating the regular man was being replaced and Mack Scott was standing in for him.

As he waited the Executioner surveyed the big plane's interior. It was jammed with equipment, including a high-powered generator near the back that already was humming, powered by a diesel engine with exterior exhaust. There were bolted-down swivel chairs in front of a bank of CRT screens along one side of the plane, and a row of bucket seats along the other. Most of the space was filled with instruments, large black boxes that had been made to be removed, though they had been in place for a long time.

The Plexiglas panels on each side were closed and locked as the rest of the operational personnel came on board. Dr. Peterson checked each man, talked with him a moment and sent him to his station. Eight men were involved. One had a set of target screens in video, and a corresponding set in radar. Chase planes around the target would send video pictures of the chase, the flight of the missile and the hoped-for hit by the laser beam.

Two other men controlled the laser weapon itself. To Bolan it seemed remarkably small, the size of a .50-caliber machine gun, with a turret-type operation that would rotate 360 degrees so it could fire from either side of the KC-135. One of these operators would trigger the firing button.

Others in the team worked on readout screens and gauges that represented the power supply, peak output readiness, direction and distance. One screen showed target lock-on.

It was a team operation. All the technicians were civilians, and there was a spirit of togetherness that Bolan had not seen much of lately.

Dr. Peterson spoke on the loudspeaker.

"Good morning, everyone. The official time is now 0529 hours. We shall take off exactly on time. It is your operation, Captain Cranston."

Another voice came over the system. "That's a roger, Dr. Peterson. We are now on taxi to our assigned runway for check, then with our clearance we will be under way. Have a good shot."

For the next hour they cruised around the restricted air space over the Naval Weapons Center, as the rocket-launching fighter and the chase plane went through a dry run. The mother plane, three hundred miles away, watched on its radar and video screens.

At last Dr. Peterson was satisfied. It was just before 7:00 A.M.

"Let's do it this time," Dr. Peterson said to his

own crew and the aircraft over the ocean. "This is a live test."

"Clear the ocean area, run the scans."

"Clearing," a technician said.

"Captain Cranston, let's move into our firing location just off the coast from Lompoc and Point Conception. We'll use the test corridor one mile at sea, parallel to the coast. What is our ETA?"

"Twelve minutes and twenty seconds, Dr. Peterson."

"Make final checks on laser power, operation, begin firing-countdown procedures and continue to minus fifteen seconds where we will hold."

Bolan moved around the plane. He saw the snout of the unlikely-looking laser weapon aimed toward the right-hand side of the big plane. Wrong side, he thought. Then he realized it was the direction the plane was flying that would determine from which side the shot would come.

He settled down to watch the screens. Someone had a transistor radio playing and he heard that the presidential plane was due to land at Edwards Air Force Base near Lancaster, which was between China Lake and Los Angeles, in fifteen minutes.

Bolan watched the target video monitor. It showed the missile-firing F-14 Tomcat coasting along at 400 miles per hour in a large circle. The jet fighter was awaiting orders to fire its missile on a predesignated course west over the Pacific along a specific range that had been cleared of all shipping.

The converted Boeing Stratotanker reached the

coast and turned south, its air speed reduced and the special Plexiglas screens unlocked so the laser gun could move into aiming position.

The huge aircraft was cruising at 22,000 feet in a reserved corridor. There would be no civilian airliner traffic at that altitude over those fifty square miles of sky, nor between them and the target two hundred miles at sea.

The man with the transistor passed the word that the President's destination had been changed. Air Force One was rerouted to land at LAX—Los Angeles International—instead of Edwards. There had been a nasty crash on the main runway closing that part of Edwards.

A new blip appeared on the in-plane radar. The operator motioned to Dr. Peterson.

"Looks like we have a plane well below us and slightly seaward," the operator said. "It could be Air Force One."

Dr. Peterson was everywhere. He checked the blip on the screen, saw it was at no more than two thousand feet altitude and making a preliminary approach to LAX.

He touched his intercom mike. "Captain, will you identify the aircraft at two thousand feet below us in the prohibited area."

"Roger."

Dr. Peterson frowned. He had been told of the Chief Executive's arrival at Edwards but had been assured that the Skysweeper test would not be interfered with, that they would be a hundred miles apart. But now with the President's plane coming into LAX, it could be somewhere near. The ship in the position shown on the radar screen was entirely safe. True, it was on the very edge of the danger zone, but absolutely safe. He could put a hold on the countdown until the craft below cleared the restricted zone.

A moment later the captain called back to Dr. Peterson over the earphones.

"That's a roger on the plane. It is the President. His flight had to be diverted from Edwards due to a runway crash there. He will clear the restricted area in three minutes."

"Thanks, Captain Cranston, he's out of any danger zone. We shall continue the test." Dr. Peterson looked at his crew. "All right, continue the test procedures."

The target-radar operator called out sharply. "I have Sidewinder-firing F-14 acquisition. Locking on to fighter. Ready for target Sidewinder to be fired."

Dr. Peterson nodded. "Check all monitors. Everyone should be at the fifteen-second hold on firing countdown. Radio, order the Sidewinder to be fired."

"Sidewinder fired, sir!"

"Have lock on to Sidewinder as target acquisition, ready to fire laser!" another man called.

Dr. Peterson checked his own screen, saw that the missile had been fired some two hundred miles west of them and ordered the firing countdown to continue.

Bolan stared at the business end of the laser weapon and thought it was aiming too low. It would never get two hundred miles to sea. Then he saw the target scope and checked the in-plane radar's scope. The laser was ready to fire, but at the wrong target!

"Stop the countdown!" Bolan shouted. He jumped at the gunner on the laser weapon, who had his eye to the special radar-activated scope in his sighting device, and slammed him off the chair of the laser gun.

"What the hell!" the gunner screamed, clawing to get back into position. Bolan covered the firing button with his hand and prevented anyone from touching it.

Dr. Peterson was there in five seconds.

"Mack, have you gone mad?"

"Check the target acquisition the radar man called out," Bolan said. "He's on the wrong target. He has the President's plane on his scope, not the telemetered signal from the chase plane over the target Sidewinder."

Peterson caught the operator's hands before he could cancel out the display. The target was the fast-moving blip that was below them, not the one two hundred miles at sea. Peterson was sure of it by its location on the screen.

He backhanded the radar-target operator, then brought in the backup man and told him to acquire the target over the Pacific and do it fast.

Peterson motioned to Bolan. "Mack, hold this traitor until we get off the shot, then I may throw him overboard without a parachute!"

A few seconds later the new target-acquisition

operator found the mark on the correct radar input.

"Target acquisition from the chase plane. Sidewinder, locking on. Check it please, Dr. Peterson."

Bolan bound the former radar-acquisition man's hands together behind him with electrical tape, then fastened his ankles together. Bolan stood up in time to see Dr. Peterson nod at the radar operator.

"Continue the firing countdown from five seconds. My count, four, three, two, one, fire!"

Bolan watched the gunner thumb the switch. He heard an electrical relay click. That was all. No bang, no zap, nothing.

The gunner kept his eye pressed to the soft rubber sight for two seconds. The radar man let out a whoop as the target blip vanished from his screen.

Dr. Peterson watched the video screen. Bolan looked that way. At first the Sidewinder missile was a chunk of iron pipe in the sky, then it disintegrated as the laser beam slammed through it, superheating the molecular structure of the explosive, detonating it, spraying the Pacific Ocean with metal, smoke and fire.

A cheer went up from the crew.

The chase plane over the Pacific circled the site of the hit, and the cameras followed one chunk of flaming wreckage until it splashed into the sea and sank.

Dr. Peterson stared at Bolan.

"How the hell did you know that son of a bitch was aiming the laser at the President's plane?"

"The angle. No one noticed the nozzle of this thing was pointing down at a forty-five-degree angle. I could figure out that your beam would never get two hundred miles at sea on that trajectory. Then I saw the sun glint off the plane down there and I yelled first and figured we could straighten it all out later. We needed that ten seconds."

Peterson nodded, then turned and stepped over to the man tied up on the floor and kicked him in the side.

"You bastard! You almost killed the President. We're going to have a long talk once we get on the ground. You'll tell me who you're working for, and how you knew the President would be landing at LAX instead of Edwards. You better have some good answers."

The man snorted, then laughed. Dr. Peterson kicked him in the stomach, then bent down and slapped the man's face.

The scientist got on the mike. "Everyone on board knows about the traitorous attempt. Every man is restricted to the plane when we land. We'll go directly to hangar twenty-seven. There I want an hour with my prisoner before I hand him over to the military police and Navy Intelligence, and by then the Secret Service and the FBI.

"At five this afternoon there will be a celebration in my office for the test of our longest shot. We're over the hump now. It shouldn't take us much longer to wrap up the testing. Thanks for your cooperation.''

Dr. Peterson turned to Bolan. "I'm hoping you can help me when I question the prisoner.''

"Glad you asked. I was going to volunteer for that detail.''

11

After the KC-135 was safely towed into hangar 27 and the big doors closed, Mack Bolan untaped the traitor's feet and he and Dr. Peterson walked him off the plane. Captain Cranston was left at the plane's door to make sure everyone stayed on board. Dr. Peterson told Cranston to call base security and Naval Intelligence and advise them of the serious top-secret security violation. He also told the pilot to request an interrogation team at the hangar immediately.

Dr. Peterson led Bolan and their prisoner to a twenty-foot-square room in a far corner of the hangar. It had once been used as part of an engine-testing program and was insulated with foot-thick fiberglass batting. Inside it was as quiet as a tomb.

Dr. Peterson snapped on overhead lights and slammed the door, bolting it from the inside.

The scientist turned to Bolan. "This traitor's name is Glade Hebron. He's been here since I started, and I don't know how long before that." Without a word to Hebron, Dr. Peterson hit him with a swinging backfist that staggered the slender man. Then the aging physicist summoned all his strength and followed the blow with a devastating right cross to Hebron's belly that drove him to the concrete floor.

Dr. Peterson stood over the fallen man, who still had his hands tied behind his back.

The top of Peterson's shoe caught Hebron along the side of the head with a short chopping kick that rolled the downed man from his back to his stomach. He groaned, blood tracking down his temple.

"No one will hear you, you bloody son of a bitch! You came within five seconds of shooting down the President of the United States! And it would have been my fault! I would have been on trial right along with you!"

Bolan stepped between the two.

"Hebron, how much did Smith promise to pay you to do this?"

"Didn't say for sure. At least a million, he. . . ." Only then did Hebron realize what he was telling.

"Sammy Smith said he'd pay you a million to change targets today, but how did he know the President's plane would come in at Los Angeles instead of Edwards?"

"Smith staged the crash at Edwards today. He and his friends knew the President was coming. Don't ask me how, I don't know. They set up two crashes to close the two main runways at Edwards. It was all part of another mission. They wanted the President to land at Los Angeles International. Then when this test was moved up, I got the word to go ahead. It was all chance. Everything had to work just right. If the wind was blowing the other way the President's plane would have come in on the other runway and I would have had no shot at him. Chance, it was mostly chance.''

Bolan lifted his brows. He had underestimated Smith and whoever was taking his place, probably his shadow agent.

"Did you think you could have gotten away with a shot at the wrong plane? Everyone on board would have known.''

"Hell, nobody was supposed to be watching. Everyone was too busy doing his job. I would have claimed a miss on the first try, got back on the real target, asked for another shot and hit it. The President's plane would be down and we wouldn't know anything about it until we got back.''

"Was the guy with the radio working with you?''

"Hell, no!''

Reaction too fast, Bolan noted.

"He just happened to be there, so I asked him to catch the news.''

The Executioner stepped closer.

"Who is Smith's KGB agent?''

"I don't know.''

Before the man could see it, a piston-fast punch landed in his solar plexus. Spittle laced with blood spewed from Hebron's mouth all over the room. His eyes bulged and saliva drooled down his chin as he gasped for air.

"One more chance. Who does Smith report to?''

Hebron shook his head and looked away.

Bolan stepped still closer and placed his hands on Hebron's shoulders.

"Look, don't try to be a hero now," Bolan said softly. "Save yourself any more punishment."

"Never!" Hebron screamed, and let fly a gob of spit square on Bolan's boot.

The Executioner's knee rocketed up, impacting in the man's groin. Before he could double over, Bolan held him up and glared into his face, which had now turned to a strange shade of gray.

"No more! Please, no more. I don't know who Smith works for. I got five thousand for telling him how it could be done. I got another five thousand for setting it all up so it might happen. It was part luck, getting the date changed. Then if it worked, I'd get a million in gold and three U.S. passports."

The scientist stepped forward and shouldered Bolan aside.

"Hebron, you bastard! And all the time I thought I had a team I could trust," Dr. Peterson said.

"I was in Nam, remember? That's the asshole of the world. I took more shit from more people there than I can even remember. I figure Uncle Sam owes me for the year I spent there, and I'm still going to try to collect."

"Who else on my team was helping you?"

"Nobody. I didn't need anyone. Willy was too damn dumb to do anything except bring the radio. I conned him. Anyway, I wasn't about to trust anybody, nor split the loot."

"You won't have to worry about room and board for at least thirty-five years, Hebron. Uncle Sam is going to take extra good care of you. Probably solitary most of the time. A man who tries to kill the President never lives long in prison. The other inmates take care of him."

Glade Hebron almost forgot his pain at the physicist's words.

"I'd really like to tear you apart, Hebron, save the government a trial and some sucking defense attorney a fee, but hell, I'm getting too old for the fun and games part. Let's move."

When they got back to the plane, they found Marine guards surrounding it. All had loaded M-16s. A lieutenant came up and saluted Dr. Peterson. He made a quick verbal report, then Dr. Peterson told those on the plane the good news.

"Men, we all have a mandatory debriefing by Naval Intelligence. Hebron's little play upstairs is the subject, and I want you all to tell it exactly the way it happened."

By the time the crew got off the plane a table and a dozen folding chairs had been set up. Two men in dark blue suits took the test crew one at a time, starting with the ones farthest from the action, the two pilots and the navigator in the cockpit. The investigators tape recorded everything.

The elder of the N.I. men told each person debriefed the same thing.

"You realize this is a matter of extreme sensitivity that affects our national security. It is now your duty to forget that it ever happened and to communicate these events to no one, not even your family. To do so would put you in violation of your security clearances and direct military orders, and would open you to prosecution under the National Security Act. Under no circumstances are any members of the press to be informed.''

Bolan and Dr. Peterson were the last to be called. The test director introduced Bolan as Mack Scott.

''Gentlemen, this is a bit unusual. Mr. Scott was not a regular member of the test team. He was brought in at the last minute this morning as a replacement for a standby radio operator at my insistence, to provide us with an added element of airborne security. I took him along on my own responsibility.

''This man prevented the President from being killed today. That is the major overriding consideration. He is in the same line of work you are but is not free to reveal his branch of service nor his real name. However in this case it is results that all of us are after. We have the results we need: the President saved, the mission completed. I request to be present when you talk to Mr. Scott.''

From there on it was routine. The two Naval Intelligence men were bright, quick to see the position in which Dr. Peterson had placed himself and sympathetic to his reasons. They did not question Bolan at all about his true identity, only about the sequence of events and how he prevented the firing.

''I would assume you will not be available to

testify in court when Hebron is brought up on charges?''

"Right," Bolan said, indicating to all three that he had at one time been in the service.

"We can live with that. We have plenty to convict."

"One question, Dr. Peterson. We understand there was a minor interrogation before we arrived. How did the prisoner receive that nasty wound on the side of his head?''

"I thought you knew. He fell down the steps getting out of the aircraft.''

Both Naval Intelligence men smiled and closed the inquiry.

Bolan went back to Dr. Peterson's office with him. They had just started to look at the next series of tests when the phone rang. Dr. Peterson answered it and handed it to Bolan.

"Yes?"

"This is Kara Ralston. We have had three calls now by someone named Malia, who says you should call her right away. Is that a familiar name?''

Bolan felt his throat tighten but his voice was almost normal. "Yes, did she leave a number?''

"Each time. She sounded upset, worried, maybe frightened." The woman gave Bolan the number.

"Thanks."

"Our date still on for four o'clock this afternoon?''

Bolan frowned. "It depends. I'll try to make it,

but this could be trouble. We'd better cancel. If I can get there I'll call you."

"Hey, sounds good. Fix that problem and call me."

They said goodbye and hung up.

It all spelled trouble. Malia must have left the motel and been spotted. Kara knew where to find him and she knew they had captured Malia.

"Problems?" Dr. Peterson asked.

"Yes, I'm afraid a big one, but I hope not a deadly one. May I use your phone?"

12

Bolan heard the phone on the other end ring ten times before it was picked up. He knew it was part of their plan: waiting, threats, intimidation and then an eventual hostage trade. A man's voice came on the line.

"Uh-huh?"

"I'd like to speak to Malia. She told me to call her at this number."

"Sure, blood. I mean we got this foxy lady says she knows you. She's got short brown hair, big brown eyes and a kind of a round face. Hawaiian type. Name's Malia. You know her?"

"Yeah, so what? I know lots of women."

"True, my man, true. We think she'll work good in one of our pleasure palaces of exotic love. She's not that outstanding, know what I mean? I just made a practice run and nothing special. Dig?"

"You bought it, you feed it."

"Hey, we figured you might be interested in buying her back. Figured you was heavy with this fox."

"You figured wrong, I only met her twice. I'm new in town."

"You're new, but you're known. We got a

straight deal for you: ten thousand and you get the lady in prime condition. Otherwise she eventually winds up turkey meat.''

Bolan gripped the receiver tighter. It was getting harder and harder for him to put up the front. Even in this air-conditioned office, the Executioner felt sweat popping out on his forehead.

''Tough, I'm a steak man, myself. See you around.''

''Hold it!'' There was a touch of desperation. ''Okay, maybe that's too high. Bring five big ones and we'll deal.''

''Hell, I don't want her. Tell you what. I'll invest my poker winnings from last night, three hundred. That's all the cash I got. She may even pay me back someday. You wanna deal?''

''You musta learned to haggle to Tijuana, brother. Deal. I'll tell you how to get here.''

Bolan repeated each part of the instructions, memorizing them.

''Got it. I'll be there by five this afternoon.''

''Okay, and bring cash. I don't take no checks.''

''You got it.''

The Executioner's features resembled a mask etched in granite, and his chilling blue gaze betrayed the grim repugnance that he felt.

Bolan hung up and Dr. Peterson, who had listened to half the conversation, glanced at him.

''Who have they got?''

''Malia. She's a government agent who had been living with Sammy Smith. Now they are threatening to turn her into turkey meat. She's Defense Intelligence Agency. I need some equipment. Can you get me a grenade launcher, for an M-16?''

"Live ammo, the works?''

"Right.''

"Okay, I'll use my clout to get it. About a dozen loaded magazines for the M-16 and a dozen 40mm HE rifle grenades. Anything else?''

"A few blocks of C-4 plastique.''

"Give me half an hour. Right back here.'' He started to leave, then made a phone call and talked quietly. When he hung up he pursed his lips. "You know this is a setup, don't you? They are using the girl to draw you out.''

"I know. She may already be dead, but I have to check it out.''

"I'm going along to help.''

"No. You've got to get Operation Skysweeper finished. I'll see you right here in thirty minutes.''

Bolan got a map from Dr. Peterson's secretary and studied it. The location was north, twenty miles past Trona at the edge of the Panamint Range, which was partway into Death Valley.

The meeting point was a fork in a desert dirt road well off the highway, the voice on the phone had said. There was a highway sign marked Panamint Valley pointing toward it, which Bolan could not miss.

An ideal spot for a transfer, Bolan thought. Impossible to plant a squad since the kidnappers were already on site. But from sitting in the desert for a few hours they would be tired, hot and, he hoped, exhausted.

A plan was starting to form in his mind. By the

time Dr. Peterson returned, it was fleshed out ready to go.

The physicist had a barracks bag containing the grenade launcher, ammunition and explosives that Bolan had requested. The scientist's eyes fell on the map.

"Mack, I know that area, right next to Death Valley park. A hell of a rugged place. You go in by car and I'll take the chopper I have available, and we'll coordinate our hit on the site. We'll both have two-way radios I can get...."

Bolan held up his hand.

"Thanks, but this one is mine. I didn't get the girl involved in the game, but I didn't keep her safe after I tried, so it's my responsibility. If I don't come back your project rolls along. If you end up with a pair of .45 slugs in your brain, there will be a real hassle to finish the work here. No arguments."

As he talked Bolan checked the launcher. The 40mm grenades were the right type. He shook hands with Dr. Peterson. Then Bolan was gone.

The barracks bag was safely stowed in the trunk of Bolan's rented Ford. At the gate there was a friendly wave and he was away.

It took him nearly an hour along Highway 178, then north toward Trona, and at last he shook out the twenty miles to the sign that said Panamint Valley. He saw an unused trail that angled away to the east into the desert and dry hills toward Death Valley. Bolan stopped and considered the situation. He had no way of knowing how far it would be to the fork in the road.

The Panamint Valley road was little more than a scratch through the arid terrain, with perhaps a road-scraper blade sent over it once a year after the cloudbursts.

The moment he got on the dirt trail he would send up a plume of dust behind his rig that could be spotted for twenty miles. There was no way around it. For just a second he realized he was dealing with professionals. They knew their business. He hoped they underestimated him, and he would give them every chance of doing so.

He had the silenced Beretta 93-R hidden under a lightweight sport jacket. He nosed off the road into the dirt track toward the target valley. Bolan stopped there and took his weapons case out of the trunk. He assembled the M-16 and attached the grenade launcher. Then he fitted an HE round into the tube. Next he slapped a fresh magazine into the weapon and laid it on the seat. Six of the HE rounds came in a small plastic vest pack that could be slipped over the neck and arms. This he placed beside the M-16.

Bolan knew he was early. He moved down the road at ten miles per hour and checked behind him. There was a telltale plume of dust even at that rate, so he pushed down the pedal and hit twenty-five, which was maximum without shaking the car to bits.

The road went straight for six miles, with a road sign at each mile marker designating the "four mile road" and the "five mile road." Only there were no crossroads, not even a trail.

The route began to climb slightly. As he looked

ahead he saw the afternoon sun glinting off some highly polished metal. Chrome? He couldn't tell how far away it was. Bolan knew distances on the barren desert were difficult to estimate.

He passed the ten-mile marker and then ahead he could see the shimmering dark blob of two cars. He guessed he was still a quarter of a mile away, and instead of slowing down he gunned the Ford, jolting unmercifully over the rough road. He approached the other vehicles at fifty miles per hour and roared right past them.

As he sped by he heard a shout and a shot fired, but nothing hit his rig. Then he eased off the gas, slowed, turned around and came down the slight incline with only his eyes showing over the driver's window. He had hunched down so he could work the brake with one hand.

He stopped thirty yards away, slammed the lever to neutral and pulled on the emergency brake but left the motor running.

"Where is she?" Bolan bellowed.

A black man, stripped to the waist, emerged from behind the first car, a gray Lincoln Continental.

"Right here, man. That little woman is safe and sound. Got the cash?"

"Not yet. Show me the girl, I mean in the road, and I want to see the other gunmen you have behind those wheels."

"A cautious man."

"Live longer that way."

The black waved at the car farthest from him and Malia got out slowly, rubbing her wrists as if they had been tied. Bolan had his hand on the M-16, the snout resting on the door padding, ready to fire.

"Now the gunmen, all of them."

The black laughed and shrugged. He waved again and three men stood, one on each side of the other car, the third next to the Lincoln. Two were Mexicans, one was white. They all held handguns.

In a sweeping glance Bolan saw the road that forked to the left. When it had been made, the road grader or a bulldozer had created a minor ditch for drainage. A new plan came to him in a heartbeat.

"Come on, mother. Where's the money?" the black shouted.

Bolan had put three hundred dollars' worth of twenties together and bound them with a rubber band.

He unlatched the Ford's door and swung it out, then with his left hand he held the bundle up so they could see it. His right hand still caressed the M-16.

"All here. And this is the deal. I'll throw the package up the road. The woman picks it up and tosses it to you. Then she comes over to my wheels."

The black man grinned. "Sounds fair, man. I don't want no trouble, and the brothers don't want no mess. Clean and easy. Let her fly."

Bolan wondered if they would try a round each when he lifted up to throw, but at ninety feet it was one hell of a long pistol shot. He lobbed the bundle exactly where he wanted to, in the ditch across the little road from the men behind the cars. It hit the edge of the trail and skidded into the depression. It had to be deep enough to protect one small woman's body.

"What the—?"

"So I'm not a big-league pitcher. Send the girl to get it."

"Just stay cool, everybody," the black said. He motioned for his prisoner to move, and Malia walked to the ditch, grabbed the money and looked at Bolan.

"Throw it to them just as we agreed," he said, hoping that she could figure out the tactic he was trying. She flung the money toward the Lincoln.

Almost at the same instant Bolan lifted the M-16 and fired the grenade launcher at the black man. Then the Executioner turned the M-16 toward the other men and triggered a six-shot burst.

The HE grenade exploded just behind the first car where the black ran for protection. The Executioner heard a scream and emptied the rest of the clip. Then he ducked below the dash and slammed in a new magazine. Two slugs pierced the Ford's windshield, shattering the glass and thudding dully into the backrest of Bolan's seat.

Bolan looked over the door to where the girl lay. She was face down in the ditch, her hands over her head.

He saw one head poking out from behind the first car and Bolan sent three 5.56mm whizzers toward it. Two creased the side of the car and slanted away. The third bullet missed the car, but plowed into the gunman's right eye, almost shearing off half his face.

Bolan heard the engine of the other car roar to life, then die. He slipped another grenade into the cylinder, lifted the weapon and fired. The round went wide. The engine caught, the car backed around. Bolan reloaded and triggered the grenade launcher. This one hit the other car's front tire and exploded, the concussion momentarily lifting the vehicle, the heavy shrapnel shredding the wheel, mangling the fender and blowing off the hood.

Bolan fired two more HE rounds at the tail end of the Lincoln. The second grenade impacted the gas tank, setting the car on fire.

Only the crackling of the flames disturbed the peaceful Mojave desert. Then a human voice intruded.

"Dammit, I give up. No more fucking grenades!" The black leader stood, his hands in the air, his right arm and a slash across one thigh dripping blood.

"Where are the other three men?" the Executioner called, still not showing himself. He glanced at Malia. She was in the same position.

"Wasted, man. You win, now give me a ride into town to the damn hospital."

"Did you rape Malia?"

"What difference does that make now?"

"Did you?" Bolan pressed.

"Well, she didn't exactly agree. But you know how it is with these ladies. Say no when they mean yes."

"Damn right. I know."

Bolan triggered a six-round burst. He saw holes appear in the man's chest, surprise and anger on his face as he jolted backward and writhed in the desert for a moment, then lay still.

"Stay down, Malia!" Bolan shouted. "You okay?"

She turned and looked at him. "Yes."

Bolan had a fresh clip in and a grenade in the launcher chamber as he zigzagged from his car to the Continental. One man lay in the driver's seat, a fatal shrapnel wound just over his nose. The second man lay behind the car with three M-16 rounds in his chest. A third corpse lay halfway to the second car, which was still burning. The Executioner ran back to Malia, helped her up and they dashed to his Ford. The windshield was completely shattered, but little other damage showed.

"Let's get out of here before some curious tourist comes in to see what's burning."

He floored the accelerator, rattling over the rutted desert track until they reached the highway.

Traffic was light on the road that connected Trona with parts of Death Valley.

When they turned onto the state highway heading south, Malia started to cry. She leaned against him and sobbed into his shoulder. He had seen it happen many times. Witnessing sudden death is a jolting, terrible experience for most people. Ten miles down the road she leaned back and wiped her eyes.

"Hey, it's over. My only concern was to get you

out of the line of fire. You were a professional. You did exactly what I wanted you to."

"I think I better confess that I messed up," Malia said softly. "I didn't trust the motel phone and went out to use the pay phone across the street. Evidently somebody saw me. Those men...back there said they had checked every motel for ten miles before they found me."

"It doesn't matter now."

"Still, I admit I fouled up. It won't go in my report, but you know. Now, tell me about the test. How did it go, and what happens next?"

"The shot went perfectly. They are getting a handle on the dispersant problem. Kara Ralston was one of Smith's people. Her number was on that list in the safe. She's still deeply involved. I had a date with her at four but I'll miss it. But we still have another problem. Where do we hide you?"

"Another motel?"

"No, too obvious."

They had entered the village of Trona and Bolan pulled in at a filling station and used the telephone to call Dr. Peterson in his office. He talked with the scientist for a few minutes, then returned to the car.

"For the next few days you are going to stay at the Unmarried Women Officers' Quarters in the Naval Weapons Center."

One hour later Bolan and the DIA operative pulled into the center. Dr. Peterson escorted Malia to her new quarters and showed her the operation. There was a separate mess, and she'd be allowed to use the base facilities. But he cautioned her to stay in the room as much as possible.

Back in his office, Dr. Peterson motioned Bolan to a chair.

"We're compressing our time schedule. Dr. Ludlow and I have eliminated a week of testing. We both agree there is no need for it. We have corrected the dispersal problem as best we can without some new breakthrough."

"And all this means...."

"We've set our final test for tomorrow. Vandenberg Air Base will have a missile shot ready for us somewhere around noon. We're going to try for an air-to-air hit on a missile that will be more than three hundred miles high and two hundred miles downrange over the Pacific Ocean."

13

Mack Bolan listened to Dr. Peterson as they sat in his office at the center.

"So you expect this shot tomorrow to be the most important test of the series?"

"That's right. And I don't think the project is safe yet. I wonder what the hell the Smith crew of KGB pawns will try tomorrow?"

The Executioner stood and paced around the room. "They tried to hit us from inside and it didn't work. I'm sure they had only one man on the plane crew. Looks as if the only logical move would be to try for some kind of hit at the shot from outside."

Dr. Peterson scratched his chin. "Outside the plane?"

Bolan nodded. "If they could disable your KC-135 it would delay the shot."

Dr. Peterson picked up the phone and ordered the guards tripled on the Stratotanker. Then he hung up and looked at Bolan.

"Chase," the Executioner said. "You should have two Tomcats flying cover for you. They can slow down to your speed and monitor the air space around you all the time."

Dr. Peterson nodded and picked up the phone again. Two minutes later he smiled.

"Done. We'll have two F-14 Tomcats in the air flanking us the moment we get to ten thousand feet."

"What about your crew?"

"I have a good crew for tomorrow. Some of the people rotate. If any of them report in sick, I'll be damned careful who I pick as a replacement."

Bolan felt an old tingle. An instinct, a second sight, but Bolan had been using it for years to stay alive. It came again and he frowned slightly. Then he pounded one fist into his other open palm.

"The attack must come from outside. They know we will tighten up security inside so their backup will be an outside shot."

"Vandenberg doesn't matter. If their missile doesn't track right or blows up on the pad, we just postpone, it isn't a negative for the program. So they will hit us here. Where is the damn hole in our defenses?"

Bolan looked out the window, saw a plane lifting off from Armitage Field in the distance. A smaller form moved with it for a while, then pulled up and hovered. He snapped his fingers.

"Dr. Peterson. You said ten thousand feet is where the Tomcats will start to give you coverage. Our hole is low-level protection. From ground zero up to ten thousand. It would have to be a business jet once you got up a few thousand feet. But at low level almost anything could do you in, a rifle, a ground-to-air shoulder-mounted missile or an armed helicopter. Did you say you had a chopper available?"

"Yes, but it's unarmed."

"Could you get an Air Force Cobra gunship up here by morning?"

"We have quite a few Air Force ships here, but no reason for a Cobra. Doubt if I could get one moved in here that soon. That would take interservice work. Tough."

"Forget it. I'll fly cover for you in the chopper. I'll be in the air just before you take off. Tell your pilot to climb at maximum rate to get away from any potential groundfire."

"Captain Cranston flew in Nam, he'll put some moves on anyone on the ground. But what can you do in an unarmed bird?"

"I won't be unarmed. I still have that barracks bag of yours. Let's go out to the hangar and check on the guards around that plane."

An hour later they had been challenged three times trying to walk toward the KC 135. Once, an officer raced up in a jeep bristling with soldiers packing loaded M-16s.

Satisfied, the two men returned to the Bachelor Officers' Quarters where Dr. Peterson had arranged for two rooms for the night. After the Executioner had settled into his quarters he dialed the room where Malia was staying.

She answered on the second ring.

"Mack, good to hear from you. Nothing's happened and I still want to do something."

"We went over that. Just sit tight. You did all the preliminary work right through to this point. Now your cover is blown, so you can't expose yourself. Happens."

"I never did thank you for saving my life out there in the desert."

"There'll be enough time for that."

Bolan hung up and stared into the darkness of the Spartan room. His target was still the KGB, but in the meantime he had inherited this baby-sitting job with Dr. Peterson. He had to dig into the conspiracy and find the shadow agent, and whoever was behind it all.

The Executioner had to find them.

He had made a vow to April Rose when he cradled her in his arms after the attack on Stony Man Farm.

His mission in this life was to stamp out as much of the evil in the world as he could. The Mafia, the terrorists, and now the ultimate in human degradation and inhumanity to man, the KGB.

He would enter each confrontation with a desperation that came from knowing he was right. He was on a collision course with eternity, he knew that. But while he drew breath he would never surrender in his single-minded purpose to erode the dark forces that motivated Animal Man.

Bolan stood for everything that the KGB tried to suppress. There was no doubt in his mind that the total domination of the world was the base purpose of the KGB and the Russian dictatorship.

He closed his eyes and for just a moment he felt the cold, still form of April Rose.

Enough! Time to turn it off and get some sleep so he could function flat-out tomorrow. He had a hunch it was going to be a crucial day.

Deliberately he turned over, and tried to clear his mind. Dark images swirled, merged, smoothed and mingled with black on black.

He slept.

NEXT MORNING Bolan and Dr. Peterson were on the flight line at 6:00 A.M. The flight was set for 8:45 but they arrived early to look around. Peterson called up his chopper, a Navy version of the Hughes OH-6, basically an observation craft. Bolan met the pilot and stowed his heavy barracks bag on board.

"We'll take off twenty minutes before the test plane for a recon around the end of the runway and beyond for a mile or so," Bolan said.

The pilot nodded. "Yes, sir. Dr. Peterson informed me of the potential problem."

Bolan liked the flier. His name was Lieutenant J.G. Dan Johnson.

Dr. Peterson supervised the check of the plane and made sure only the men he authorized were on board. Then he buttoned it up and kept the exterior guards around it as he went through three dry runs of the procedure for this important shot.

Radio informed him that the missile countdown was going on schedule and blast-off was set for one hour from that moment.

Dr. Peterson gave Bolan the okay to take off, the test plane would follow in fifteen minutes. Bolan hit the concrete running and jumped into the chopper.

"Let's fly, Johnson," he said. At once the Executioner opened the barracks bag and pulled out the M-16 with grenade launcher and spotter scope attached, and stood the assembled and loaded Childers shotgun between his knees.

They received clearance from the control tower and the chopper lifted off. Bolan asked for an inspection of the runway the KC-135 would use. With the tower's permission they buzzed it twice at ten feet and found nothing suspicious. They worked out over the end of the runway, which was still well within the boundaries of the base.

The Executioner reported to Dr. Peterson that everything looked in order. A few minutes later the converted KC-135 rolled down the concrete strip.

Bolan's chopper was at one thousand feet then, and he searched the arid ground below him with a pair of binoculars. Two miles to his left near the outer zigzag fence of the center, he saw a puff of dust.

"Check out that dust devil at nine o'clock on the deck," Bolan said.

Johnson saw it and took the Hughes chopper down at a steep angle.

"Damn, that's another chopper," Johnson said. "Son of a bitch is taking off."

It came off the ground, banked and then worked in closer to the airfield as it circled to gain altitude. Bolan continued scanning the terrain. What he saw made his hands tighten on the glasses.

"She's got something strapped to her landing struts," Bolan said. "Looks like a ground-to-air missile. Close in, Johnson!"

The Executioner could see the converted Stratotanker roaring down the runway almost directly ahead of them, three miles away. He saw the chopper lift higher and his own helicopter slid down out of the sky to intercept the slightly larger, civilian craft.

Bolan checked the landing skids again with his binoculars, and this time he saw the fins and the special nose cone.

"It's a heat-seeking missile, sure as hell," Bolan said. He grabbed the mike to warn the KC-135 to abort the takeoff, but he was too late. The huge aircraft below gained flying speed and lifted off, heading straight at them and climbing sharply.

"Keep that ship coming straight ahead!" Bolan yelled into the mike, but he was not sure it got through. If the big plane turned at right angles either way, the chopper slightly below it could turn and get a broadside shot at the converted tanker.

"Close the gap on that killer bird!" the Executioner shouted.

"I'm using full throttle!" the pilot said.

Bolan pulled up the M-16 and triggered a six-round burst at the civilian helicopter. The door on Bolan's chopper had been removed for ease of observation. The rounds would fall short.

He waited and watched as the big KC-135 roared toward them with all four jets screaming, clawing for power to pull the tons of metal higher into the sky.

Then the huge airship started to bank. She would be less than half a mile from the enemy chopper below when she made the turn, and broadside.

They were closer now. Bolan fired three rounds and saw them slap into the aft section of the chopper. The tail section waggled, then the pilot slanted away downwind and out of the best firing position on the KC-135. But Bolan knew position didn't matter that much now. Given the approximate direction, the heat-seeking nose cone on the killer missile would do its own aiming as it homed in on the screaming superheated jet engines.

Bolan fired again until the M-16 magazine went dry. He saw one hit and again the bird faded downwind. A window in the back of the chopper cabin opened and winks of gunfire showed there.

"Get me closer!" the Executioner shouted over the noise of the helicopter.

"Only way is to get on top of them," the pilot called.

Bolan nodded and the pilot climbed, worked forward slowly to a position about a hundred feet over the top of the enemy bird before the other pilot could see where his attacker had vanished.

Bolan changed weapons, took the Childers and motioned for Johnson to settle lower over the bird. The civilian pilot must have sensed where the other craft was, as he made several moves to throw off the Navy chopper.

But Johnson stayed with the craft and was now less than fifty feet over the bird and drifting down. Bolan fired one round from the Childers.

"Lower!"

Johnson dropped his bird another thirty feet until they could read the stenciled warnings on the roof below. There Bolan held the Childers in an iron grip and fired straight down into the top of the chopper cabin.

The slugs ripped into the roof of the chopper. Suddenly the civilian helicopter slanted to the left and began plummeting out of control toward the earth.

The missile detonated on impact and a large yellow ball of flame mushroomed off the desert, followed by thick black smoke as the civilian chopper and its fuel supply exploded.

Bolan watched the spot as his helicopter circled at two hundred feet. He took the mike and punched the button.

"KC-135 Peterson, you are cleared from chopper one to continue your mission. We are out of visual with you. The Tomcats should pick you up shortly."

"Roger, Hughes-one. Did we see a second chopper near the boundary line of the center?"

"Right, you did. But you can scratch that chopper with its heat-seeking missile. It is no longer a factor. Good luck on your shot."

Johnson took the mike and called in a Navy crash-site team to set up security around the wreckage until the appropriate authorities were notified. He and Bolan took one last look at the jumbled, blackened mass and knew nothing could be alive inside.

Almost an hour later as Bolan sat in Dr. Peterson's office, the radio contact came through.

"Shot just completed, exactly on time. Radar shows a one hundred percent successful test. Target destroyed 340 miles altitude and 256 miles down Pacific range."

Bolan sipped the coffee he had been provided with and then stood. Everyone in the office was cheering and slapping one another on the back.

The Executioner slipped quietly out the door and headed toward his car.

As he drove, Bolan wondered if this was the last test, and if the project was over. If so, he still had to find the shadow agent, only now it would be harder.

14

Joseph Vishnevetsky sat brooding in his fortified house on Windward Street. Four hours ago he had heard that his chopper had been shot down. It was supposed to wipe out the KC-135, all of its test components and its crew. Crashing the KC-135 would have set back Operation Skysweeper a year. Now the shot had been completed, he had lost two men and the helicopter and the whole program was almost wrapped up.

"Activate," he said softly to himself. There was no other way. Now was the time to activate and see if the system really worked. There had been several positive results so far in the long program.

Vishnevetsky descended the stairs to the basement. He walked to the safe concealed behind a movable paneled wall, opened it and took out a yellowed document. He began to read it. It was a complete report on the "debriefing and retraining" of one Lieutenant Roth Ludlow at the Hanoi Hilton late in the Vietnam war.

Ludlow had been the most responsive of the students in the program, which had involved more than two hundred American officers. Vishnevetsky read again the key activation words, smiled and returned the material to the safe.

Upstairs he checked his watch. Almost 5:00 P.M. Ludlow was probably still at his desk. He had a habit of working until six or seven o'clock. Vishnevetsky picked up the handset and dialed.

"Good afternoon, Dr. Ludlow's office."

It was Kara. Vishnevetsky smiled. "Is he in? I need to speak with Dr. Ludlow."

"Yes, sir, I'll put you right through."

Vishnevetsky heard a few clicks, then the phone was picked up on the first ring.

"Ludlow here."

"Baseball needs Roth Ludlow," Vishnevetsky said, using the trigger words that had been beaten into Ludlow's subconscious so many years before in Hanoi.

"What did you say?"

"Baseball needs Roth Ludlow. You will call this number in two hours exactly: 375-4444. Remember that number." And Vishnevetsky repeated the numbers.

ROTH LUDLOW wrote 375-4444 on his note pad. Then the line went dead. He hung up the phone and shivered.

Quietly he repeated the words. "Baseball needs Roth Ludlow." He said them ten times, then told Kara he was leaving for the day and left his office through a rear exit. He seldom did that.

Ludlow drove home in a daze. At his house he sat in his den and stared at the wall. Far-off images began to appear on the white wall and he saw the jungles of Vietnam float in. He felt the heat and the constant humidity and slapped a mosquito.

He ducked under a branch and the small Oriental behind jabbed at him with a rifle. Ludlow hurried down the trail.

The prison camp had been pure agony. He lived through bits of it again, and then he was in the room with Dr. Moskalenko. The kind-looking colonel was talking softly to him and Ludlow had to listen carefully to hear all the words.

"Baseball needs Roth Ludlow."

"Yes," Ludlow said. "Baseball does need Roth Ludlow, but will it ever give me a chance?"

"Roth Ludlow will be given a chance to play. He must only wait for his call. Wait for his call. Wait for his call."

Then Ludlow was back in the whitewashed room with no windows and the metal bucket over his head, his hands tied behind him. Two men kept pounding on the bucket with thin metal rods. There was no actual physical damage, but the constant battering of metal on metal slowly drove him out of his mind. Just before he collapsed they stopped and pushed him under a cold shower, then fed him a glorious meal and brought in a small Chinese woman for him.

Ludlow was so detached, so fearful, so cowed that he could do nothing but sit and watch as the woman undressed and tried to seduce him without success.

Roth Ludlow shook his head.

"No, dammit, no! I am not in Vietnam! I am not in Vietnam! I am in Ridgecrest, California. I work at the Naval Weapons Center. I am head of Operation Skysweeper!" He heard his wife come into the room and it took him several moments to focus on her. The jungles of Vietnam faded and he tried to relax.

"Tough day?" she asked.

He nodded. She had seen him in one of his mind flashes and understood. She was a trained psychologist. She put some music on his stereo cassette deck and he tried to relax.

"I'll work it out," he said and she nodded and left, knowing he wanted to struggle with it by himself. She went downstairs, used the other line and called Dr. Urick at the Branch Clinic at the center. Quickly she filled him in on the little she had heard.

"It's not a usual mind flash, doctor, but close. He is having a tremendous battle with his subconscious, I would say. I have no idea why, and you know he never talks about it." She listened for a few moments. "Yes, I know. Whatever we can do to make him well again is what we're after."

Beth Ludlow hung up with a deep frown. She came back upstairs to the den and stood there looking at her husband.

Roth Ludlow lifted his head and saw his wife standing at the door. He felt something grating on him. He had a phone call just before he left the office, but he could not remember what it had been about. What was it? He tried but it would not surface. Probably unimportant.

Where did this sudden feeling of tension come from? He felt he was ready to blow up, as though there was something he had to do but he was not quite sure what it was.

Again and again his experiences in Vietnam flashed into his mind, and he thought about that ridiculous colonel who had been so nice toward the end. For a while there Roth almost believed that Moskalenko would help him and the other prisoners. But he never did, just talked and talked. One of the other captured American officers said he was sure the Russian colonel was trying to hypnotize Ludlow. But he did not let it happen and a few days later they stopped taking him in for his retraining interviews.

Now Ludlow shook his head. What was the matter with him? He had a dozen big jobs waiting for him on his desk, and here he was at home thinking about what happened thirteen years ago.

Ridiculous! He should go right back to the office and get to work. He felt a sudden pain in his stomach and he bent over to relieve it. What in the world was that? He remembered a few similar pains when he was at the Hanoi Hilton, but he had not even thought of them in years.

"Baseball needs Roth Ludlow, phone 375-4444." He said the words out loud and frowned. Now what in hell did they mean? Baseball needs Roth Ludlow? Ridiculous. Sure, he had played ball in high school and then in college, but he was not a star, not about to be drafted by a major league club.

The more he thought of the phrase the more familiar it sounded. He repeated it in his mind, then gradually said it again and again until he could think of nothing else. After ten minutes of saying the words over and over in his mind, he sat down at his desk and dialed the number.

When the phone rang on the other end he pressed the receiver tightly to his ear. Sweat popped out on his forehead and a small rivulet coursed down his nose.

"Yes?"

"My name is Roth Ludlow, First Lieutenant, United States Air Force. Serial number 542-24-7706-FR."

"Very good, Lieutenant Ludlow. You will leave your home, tell your wife you are going out for some new headache pills you heard advertised. Then come directly to 1444 Windward and ring the front door bell three times. You will be met. You are doing extremely well in this test, Lieutenant. Remember, come at once, make the excuse to your wife and hurry, we have many miles to travel before daylight."

Ten minutes later Ludlow stopped his car in front of the house on Windward. He was met by a man who asked for his keys. Ludlow watched while his car was driven through a gate and into an attached garage and the door closed. Then they went into the house.

A small balding man with fat pink cheeks met him and nodded curtly.

"Dr. Ludlow! It's so good to meet you at last. My name is Moskalenko, you may remember me from your past. Now, we have much work to do."

Vishnevetsky used the Moskalenko name to re-inforce the programming. Now he saw that Ludlow had dropped into a deep hypnotic trance as a result of the trigger words. He had made the phone call and used his own name and former rank and serial number, which further deepened the hypnotic trance. He was ready for his instructions.

Vishnevetsky led the physicist to the basement, beside the soundproof target range and into another room where a variety of lights, slides and other instruments had been assembled.

The lights were dimmed and Ludlow was shown a series of TV clips and movie film on some of the worst sequences to come out of the Vietnam war. In one, women and children ran in flames from napalmed huts. Living color showed blood pouring from military and civilian casualties. Twisted charred corpses of human beings were displayed. A dramatic shot of a U.S. Air Force plane strafing, bombing and napalming a target that appeared to be a hospital plainly marked with a red cross, came on the screen.

Ludlow sat through the five-minute film without a change of expression. Then Vishnevetsky went through some of the same series of hypnosis-deepening exercises that Ludlow had experienced in the Hanoi Hilton.

There followed a break for Cokes and doughnuts, then back to the training.

"Lieutenant Ludlow, you will answer the following questions to the best of your ability, holding back nothing. How did the testing go today with the missile shot?"

"Perfectly. It was a total success. We have achieved all of the test parameters we set out to complete."

"What is the next step in Operation Skysweeper?"

"We will finalize the hardware, further develop our actual laser nozzle and continue a program of refinements on containing the dispersant qualities of the beam itself."

"The actual hardware, the beam technology and the firing apparatus are all finished testing and ready for application?"

"That is correct."

"What is your estimation of the date when these satellites could be in operational orbit?"

"That is not a part of my task. I have no idea."

"This man working with you, Mack Scott. Who is he?"

"I am not sure. He isn't CIA or DIA or he would have said so. That is what Peterson tells me."

"Where is he staying?"

"I have no idea."

"Thank you, Lieutenant, you are doing extremely well. Now I will give you some suggestions, some orders. You will listen and memorize them carefully. When I am done here, you will proceed to your office and carry them out. You will be cheerful and optimistic, you will be pleasant and you will do everything you are instructed. Do you understand?"

"Yes, sir!"

"Fine. The first thing you will do tomorrow morning will be to shave and dress carefully here from clothes provided. Then you will go to your office at the usual time. . . . ''

15

Dr. Roth Ludlow got out of his car in the parking lot and walked briskly to his office. Kara, his secretary, had an especially bright smile for him this morning and he felt unusually full of vigor. He had so much to get done today, and he was going to jump on it with relish.

His first move was to unlock the three top-secret steel files and remove the bar rods that went through the drawer handles.

He looked at the files and frowned, then touched his intercom and asked Kara to come in.

"I'm putting together a comprehensive file on the complete Skysweeper project," he told her. "I want you to help me. You start on the first file and work forward. Pick out only the most important test results, the foundation research and development, that sort of thing. Reduce each of those file drawers by two thirds, but keep the vital information. I'll start on this one and work backward. We have only two hours so let's not sit on our hands."

"Yes, sir! I'll get a couple of boxes from the storeroom."

"Good idea. Now, let's move!"

OUTSIDE, THE EXECUTIONER sat in his rented Ford. The weapons were stashed in the trunk, including the M-16 with the 40mm grenade launcher and the spotter scope attached.

The previous evening he had enjoyed an interesting two-hour dinner with Malia, then taken her back to her room at the officers' quarters and driven past Dr. Ludlow's house in Ridgecrest.

He had an uneasy feeling and wanted to talk to the project director about it. Something was wrong, but he could not pin it down. When he knocked on Dr. Ludlow's door, his wife answered. She had been crying. It was a little after nine in the evening, and Dr. Ludlow was not there.

She told Bolan that her husband had made a phone call earlier that evening and talked for a while, then he told her he had to go to the store for a minute. He had not come back after more than two hours. Bolan had asked to look at Dr. Ludlow's desk, and that was where the Executioner saw the number scratched on a pad of paper: 375-4444. That was the number of the special KGB house. He told Mrs. Ludlow he knew the number and would check up on her husband.

Then Bolan drove to the house on Windward Street. Lights showed, but there was no one going in or out. No cars entered the chain link fence guarding the driveway.

The Executioner sat across the street and watched. By midnight he decided there would be little action until morning. Dr. Ludlow was probably a hostage. There would be a note tomorrow concerning a trade of the entire Skysweeper package for Dr. Ludlow's live body. At least Bolan knew where the hostage was held.

Bolan sat up in a comfortable position and went into patrol sleep, that combat state where the body is resting but half of the mind is alert, the eyes open and reacting but the signals downgraded to minor images to the brain. Any unusual noise, movement or touch brings the man back to full alert with no grogginess.

Twice during the night cars drove past the house and Bolan was alert at once, but they kept moving, just some late-night types getting home.

The Executioner was surprised just before eight that morning when Dr. Ludlow came through the front door alone, opened the garage, backed out his car and drove away. As soon as the garage door closed, Bolan followed the big Cadillac. He was surprised again when the car drove straight to the Naval Weapons Center and Dr. Ludlow parked in his usual spot outside the Lauritsen Laboratories where the major research was done on lasers and related optical systems.

Bolan found the nearest phone, called Ludlow's wife to inform her that her husband was well, safe and at work. Then Bolan hung up and dialed Dr. Peterson's number.

"I need that pilot and the chopper waiting on the near edge of the airfield. I've a hunch we'll need it."

"Take care of it in a minute. Then I'll stop by Roth's office and see if he'll tell me what is going on. If I can get anything out of him I'll take a walk over to your Ford. I can see where you're parked. Hold tight."

Bolan returned to his car and waited. Just past

ten-thirty, the Executioner saw Dr. Ludlow come from a door on the side of the building closest to his car. He carried a cardboard box, and behind him was Kara with a smaller carton. She was struggling to carry it. They put both boxes in the back seat of the light blue Caddy, and then Ludlow got in and drove away.

Bolan was getting itchy to move. It had to be a payoff, the plans, the test results, probably in exchange for Ludlow's family. It did not matter as long as it led Bolan to the KGB agent behind this whole spy operation.

A moment later Dr. Peterson came running around the building from the other side and waved at Bolan. He rushed up to the Ford and jumped in the passenger seat.

"Something is happening. Roth took about half of his files with him. He seemed strange. Hope you've got your badges on, in case we need to get into Armitage Field."

Bolan followed the Caddy down North Knox to Blandy. The lead car made a right turn and continued to Sandquist Road and turned right again. It was the quickest route to the airfield. Just past E Street they came to the security gate, flashed their badges and moved on through only two car lengths behind the Cadillac.

Bolan had briefed Dr. Peterson on what had happened the previous night with Dr. Ludlow.

"As far as I can tell the place is a safehouse for the KGB operation here, but I can't be sure. Guard dogs, electrified chain link fence give a pretty good clue."

"When I talked with Roth he was unusually closemouthed, hardly said a word," Dr. Peterson reported. "But I saw that he was gutting his files, taking the absolutely essential parts of the research and the hardware construction for the laser gun. He's moving it somewhere and this isn't at all like him. Somehow he seemed different."

They came to the field and the Caddy drove to the side away from the big hangars and toward the north end of the main runway. A blue and white helicopter sat there, its engine warmed up and the rotor spinning slowly.

A Marine guard held up his hand as a jet fighter with part of the cowl removed was towed across the street to another hangar by a powerful little electric mule. Bolan stopped until the craft was past.

"No chance to get there in time to stop the take-off," Bolan said. "Not even if I wanted to. Where is that bird we used yesterday?"

It was a quarter of a mile ahead. They got to it just as they saw the blue and white chopper lift off the pad.

The Executioner drove on to where the helicopter sat and left the car with Dr. Peterson. He grabbed the dark green barracks bag and ran for the chopper.

The Executioner threw the bag into the bird and jumped in.

"Let's move!" Bolan shouted and snapped his seat belt in place. He noticed that they hadn't yet replaced the passenger-side door. A moment later they were lifting off, the pilot talking quickly to the tower, not asking for clearance, just notifying them that he was in pursuit of the chopper that had just left the field.

The bird slanted to the left just over the buildings and they spotted the other chopper well to the west, charging across restricted areas in a mad dash for distance. Bolan's pilot, Lieutenant Dan Johnson, followed.

The chase soon developed into a standoff. Johnson had his bird at full throttle, but he could not catch the other, slightly more powerful craft. But the blue and white bird was not fast enough to lose them. They soon crossed the fence that marked the western boundary of the center.

"Can't figure out where he's going," Johnson said. "Nothing out here but sagebrush, cactus and about a thousand rattlesnakes per square mile."

As Bolan looked west he saw something else: the Sierra Nevada mountains rising up sharply from the valley. It would take a lot of skill to get over them in the choppers. The other bird slowed and began circling.

"What now?" Johnson asked.

"Dr. Ludlow's on board, so we can't shoot them down. Let's move up and see what kind of a reception we get."

They could see the pilot's door on the other craft had been removed, and before they were in range they saw pinpoint flashes winking from the cabin. Gunshots.

Johnson brought his craft down and behind the other bird to avoid being hit.

"What the hell do we do now?" Johnson asked.

"Wait. They have to be meeting someone here. If nothing else happens we force them down."

"How?"

"A couple of good slugs into that engine area should do it. Just disable the chopper and force it down without shooting them out of the sky in flames."

"Tricky. Our altitude is fifteen hundred."

"We wait five minutes."

They cruised around, keeping the blue and white helicopter in sight but staying out of range. Then Bolan asked Johnson to come in from behind. At two hundred yards he asked the pilot to swing around on the right-hand side of the other chopper. He decided on four single shots from the M-16.

Johnson pulled his bird around, came down from above and behind and then swung to the right for Bolan to get a side shot. The Executioner fired from slightly to the rear of the chopper and saw all four of his rounds slam into the engine area.

At once black smoke started trailing the stricken bird, and it wavered, lost some of its power and began falling to the ground, its big rotors still turning but with less speed now. The engine maintained just enough energy to keep the helicopter from free-falling, until it was ten feet from the ground. Then the rotors stopped and it dropped to a crash landing.

Bolan's pilot had followed it down and when it hit, Bolan indicated he should set down.

"When I jump out you get the hell out of here," Bolan shouted. "Pick me up later."

"Yes, sir," Johnson said.

When Bolan stepped out of the bird, the desert heat hit him like the inside of a pizza oven turned on high. Bolan grabbed the barracks bag and the M-16 and ran forward to a small depression fifty yards from the crashed chopper. He bellied down and peered over the crest past a gnarled sagebrush plant.

At first there was no movement, then he saw through the pilot's open door a form begin to worm out of the chopper. The craft looked fairly intact except for one broken skid that let it keel over to the left.

The pilot got out, waving a pistol. The Executioner brought up the M-16 and sent three rounds into his chest. The man screamed but the sound ended in a froth of red bubbles as he sat down quickly, then threw his hands upward and fell over on his back.

Bolan was out of his protective hole now and running hard for the downed craft. He had seen nothing of Dr. Ludlow. At the chopper Bolan ducked under it and came up on the passenger side. Ludlow was still in his seat. The belt had prevented any serious injury, but he had a bruise on his head and seemed to be unconscious. Bolan shook him. His eyes flickered open.

"What the hell?"

"Dr. Ludlow, we have to get you out of here."

"What?"

Bolan unsnapped the seat belt and pulled the scientist's legs out the door, then he found enough strength to come out by himself. He shook his head.

"What the hell am I doing out here? Who are you?"

Before the Executioner could answer, they heard automatic rifle fire and a half a dozen rounds slammed into the helicopter. Bolan grabbed Ludlow and dragged him to the ground behind the craft.

More shots peppered the aircraft and Bolan stood and peered around the broken bird. He saw another chopper in stationary hover about a hundred yards away.

"Company," Bolan said. "Were you supposed to meet someone out here?"

"I don't know. I don't remember anything about this. I don't even remember coming to work this morning!"

"Were you in Nam?" Bolan asked.

"Yes, Air Force pilot, then a POW for a while. Escaped."

"Were you in the Hanoi Hilton?"

"Right, how did you know?"

"Did they say anything about 'retraining'?"

"Yes, they tried. Bunch of hogwash."

"Keep believing that."

The chopper attacked. It roared at them less than fifty feet off the ground, and this time two automatic rifles blasted at them with full clips as the bird swooped overhead, then hung on its blades and came around for another charge. Bolan emptied the M-16 into the bird but it had no effect. He unhooked the Beretta 93-R and handed it to Dr. Ludlow.

He flicked it to auto fire and began blasting

away at the chopper. It moved off two hundred yards and settled to the ground, hidden, except for the rotors, in a small watercourse.

"Dr. Ludlow, you took some boxes from your office. What is in them?"

Dr. Ludlow shook his head, leaned in the door of the craft and leafed through the files.

"Hell, the entire file on Operation Skysweeper. What is it doing out here?"

"You brought it. But I'd guess you were under some kind of mind control. Now all we have to do is stop those men in that bird from getting these documents."

Bolan had given the scientist four loaded magazines for the Beretta.

Dr. Roth Ludlow shivered.

"Damn, what a mess. We've got to get out of here. We're gonna have gooks all over us in ten minutes. See that stream over there? If we work down it we can move faster than through this damn jungle. Come on, let's move! We've got to get all the way to Hue, before we find any kind of friendlies. Move it, you guys, you want to go back to that fucking prison in Hanoi?"

Before Bolan could stop him, Dr. Ludlow darted around the back of the chopper and took off into the desert.

16

A four-passenger Bell civilian helicopter had been circling at five thousand feet just beyond the crashed chopper. Joseph Vishnevetsky trained powerful binoculars on the ground and nodded.

"It is time for us to go down, Comrade General. I believe the pilot is dead and it looks as if Dr. Ludlow is injured in some way. There is another man down there and he is armed. It is difficult to tell what Dr. Ludlow might do in his mental state. We shall go down, eliminate both Americans, take the plans and rush you back to your submarine."

The other passenger in the helicopter grunted. He was a large man with broad shoulders, a trim body despite his fifty-odd years and a forehead that kept enlarging year after year as his hairline receded. His iron-gray hair was cut short. His pale blue eyes were wide set in a face that was smoothly shaved and lean. He prided himself on his athletic appearance.

The man was Major General Greb Strakhov, and he had been following this Operation Skysweeper from its inception. One of his major interests was antimissile defense, and he knew the Americans had stumbled onto something. Now he had to steal the whole package.

He looked at Vishnevetsky and lifted his brows. The man certainly didn't look like one of the best KGB field agents that Mother Russia had. He seemed more like a bookstore owner. But Strakhov knew the man's record and his credentials, as well as his family, his education and his political connections. He was the right person for this job. And if he succeeded he would be brought back and honored.

Now what Strakhov wanted were those plans from the downed helicopter below. It should be a simple matter. He had been two weeks in the submarine moving into position and then waiting offshore, dodging American antisubmarine patrols.

If all went well here today, he would be on his way home within hours. Yes, he had been away too long. He missed his dacha on the Black Sea coast. This was the best time of the year up there.

"Do we go down, comrade? We are armed."

Vishnevetsky bobbed his head and told the pilot to go down and hold at a hundred feet so they could use the rifles.

They came down in wide circles. When they were one hundred yards away at one hundred feet altitude, they came in straight at the man on the ground, who huddled behind the downed chopper for protection. Both Vishnevetsky and Strakhov fired AK-47s as they swung in toward the figure. They dived behind the wreckage and then moved to the far side as the Bell roared above the target at fifty feet. The bird swung around for another run.

"No!" Strakhov said. "No more firing from

here. We might ignite the wreckage and ruin the records and plans. Land, we shall dig them out on foot."

Vishnevetsky paled. "I was never much of a foot soldier, Comrade General."

"Then you shall have to learn fast. Set it down quickly, pilot. Over there in that low spot. You stay with the aircraft, and do not let the American circle around us and capture you. Kill him if he comes this way."

"Yes, Comrade General."

"Good man."

The craft touched its long landing runners on the ground and Strakhov leaped out and pointed to a small depression in the desert.

"Vishnevetsky, get over there and when you hear me firing, you come in from that side toward the helicopter. Use your cover. When you see me move forward, you fire into the craft over there. When I am in place, I will give you covering fire as you move up. Run!"

Vishnevetsky had never felt so miserable in his life. He could fire the weapon but did not like to. He knew infantry tactics but had not played at soldiering for fifteen years. But he ran.

MACK BOLAN SURVEYED THE ENEMY. The other chopper the two men had come in was well within range of his rifle grenades. But he would need to move to a better location for a good shot into the gully. He could hose down the helicopter with the M-16 and disable it. But he had a more immediate problem. The men had separated and dropped behind small sand dunes so he could not see them. They evidently were trained soldiers.

The man who ran from the chopper first was getting into easy grenade range. Bolan dug into his barracks bag, took out three of the 40mm rifle grenades and loaded one. He watched the spot where the man had vanished, and waited. The enemy who was to become Bolan's first target ran forward again, sliding behind a smaller dune. But this time Bolan could see one leg. He lifted the M-16, braced it in the sand, elevated the barrel for the distance and squeezed the forward trigger.

The round soared into the air and exploded on impact twenty yards beyond the target. Bolan had loaded a second round as he watched the first one fly. Now he lowered the angle of the barrel slightly and fired again. This round blasted the small mound of sand, and Bolan heard a cry and then a scream in the silent desert heat.

The man stood up and began limping back toward the civilian helicopter. Twice he turned around and fired at the chopper Bolan was using as cover. Bolan put the M-16 on full automatic and sent five blistering rounds at the figure. Bolan could see the sand geysering as the rounds fell short and he lifted his sights and blasted five more rounds. At least two of them hit the man, who now shouted at Bolan and tried to fire again.

New fire came from another sand dune to the left, covering the first man's retreat. Bolan ignored it and sent a ten-shot burst toward the limping man.

Six of the rounds caught Joseph Vishnevetsky.

Three slashed through his chest, pulping vital arteries and ripping into his lungs. The other three traced a pattern up his head, one of them boring in just past his Adam's apple and missing his spinal cord by a millimeter. Another slug broke out three front teeth, shattered and tore up half of his upper palate. The last round ripped through his forehead, flattened as it entered his cranial cavity and took a four-inch square of brain tissue and scalp off his head as it exited.

Bolan had seen a figure charge forward as he fired at the wounded man. Now the Executioner concentrated on the second man. He had bolted forward another fifty feet until he was little more than thirty yards from Bolan's cover. The man dived behind a six-foot-high pile of igneous rocks.

"Give it up, American, your cause is lost. You have no transport."

The Executioner listened to the Russian-accented English, and shouted back.

"I can blow up your chopper anytime."

Bolan triggered a burst of death messengers toward the rocks. Some of them plowed into the sand, some whined off into the desert.

The Executioner slipped another grenade in the launcher tube attached to the M-16 and fired at the chopper. He might get some spray shrapnel hits. The round landed short. At once the blades began spinning faster and the bird slowly rose from the ground.

Bolan moved his hand back to the M-16's trigger and aimed at the bird, but he had to duck for cover again as a dozen rounds from the Russian's automatic rifle peppered the heavy skin of the crashed craft.

When Bolan looked up, the enemy chopper was skimming the desert, rapidly moving out of range.

"Now it is just you and me, American."

"Not quite. My partner is coming up behind you."

Strakhov laughed. "Not a chance, American. The man is Dr. Ludlow, and he is so brainwashed that he can hardly think for himself, let alone respond to orders from someone else."

As Strakhov spoke, Bolan loaded another grenade and fired at the pile of rocks. Bolan was hoping the impact would send a shower of shrapnel behind the rocks if he found the right range.

A hot silence followed the blast. Bluffing, Bolan decided. He saw slight movement of desert grass near one of the stones, and Bolan sent six 5.56mm lead hornets into the spot.

Again, silence.

Bolan fired another HE round into the same spot as before.

Nothing.

He checked the barracks bag and discovered only four rifle grenades left. He slung the Childers onto his shoulder and reached for one of the remaining white phosphorous explosives. What little wind there was in the blistering desert terrain was blowing slightly away from him, toward the Russian. He shoved the phosphorous round into the cylinder and triggered the launcher at the rock pile. As the smoke billowed out and covered the stones, Bolan was up, dashing forward, the M-16 hybrid on full automatic.

Quickly he crossed the distance to the rock heap, but found no one hidden there.

"Damn," Bolan muttered.

The Russian had used the rocks as cover and moved in a direct line away from Bolan. Fifty yards ahead there was a small dry watercourse that had carved a depression in the desert after some long forgotten rainstorm.

Where the hell was the Russian?

And where was Dr. Ludlow? Without any water the scientist could get lost and die out here on the desert after as little as two hours.

The Executioner wiped sweat from his forehead as he squinted up into the unforgiving sun. He guessed the temperature to be above 100 degrees.

He looked over the protective rocks again, then swept the land on each side in a 180-degree arc. Was the enemy trying to work back to the downed chopper and its treasure? The watercourse meandered ahead, and he could see how it soon deepened and curved to the left. Maybe he could cut the Russian off by charging straight across toward the bend of the gully. Bolan nodded. Worth a try. He gripped the Childers on its sling and emerged from the rocks on a run, angling at a forty-five-degree line to where he guessed the Russian had headed.

Bolan jogged for a hundred yards, and could see the side of the six-foot-deep arroyo. He heard a chopper coming in but at first did not worry about it. He expected it to be the Navy craft flown by Lieutenant Johnson. At the last moment he looked up and saw the blue and white bird. He dived to the sand and rolled to the left just as he heard the rifle fire from above.

The rounds missed and he turned on his back and sent a dozen bullets at the bird from his M-16. Some of the slugs scored and the chopper veered off to the left. Sweat glistened on his forehead.

For the moment he was safe—but now the Russian in the gully knew where he was. Bolan worked ahead to the edge of the ravine and looked up and down it. He could see fifty yards downstream, but only about twenty to a curve the other way. There was no one there. He stood for a moment, then dropped to the sand.

The Russian grabbed at the bait. Three angry whizzers whined inches over Bolan's head and he rolled away from the lip. The shots came from upstream, past the bend in the gully. He had a direction.

Bolan crouched low and ran upstream twenty feet back from the edge of the drop-off. At the bend in the ravine, the desert runoff had exposed a cavernlike jumble of rocks forming a perfect fortress. He worked his way cautiously to the edge of the arroyo, coming up behind a thick healthy sage brush.

The rocks were strewed along the bottom of the watercourse, and many had tumbled down from the sides as the water undercut them. But to the left side Bolan glimpsed what appeared to be a tunnel or a small cave.

It struck Bolan that the enemy chopper could work back and get the Skysweeper plans while the Executioner was chasing the Russian.

He considered this as he waited. The man down there must make a move sooner or later.

Bolan dismissed the thought as his gaze swept to the downed aircraft. The blue and white chopper would not come in after the papers. The crash site was still well within M-16 range.

Bolan leaned out and sent six rounds into the dark hole among the rocks, then rolled back from the lip.

When the sound of the shots echoed away downstream, the Executioner heard a laugh.

"Missed, American, but a good try. You remind me of a man who bothered us for a long time: John Phoenix. But we disgraced him, broke him."

Bolan's throat felt so tight he did not think he could speak. He swallowed a dozen times, then moved closer to the rim. He could see no corpse among the rocks.

Was it possible? He closed his eyes, remembering the unseeing gaze of April Rose. He gripped the rifle. It was possible. This was a KGB operation, and the local man would have contact with some higher-up. But would the head of the KGB's Thirteenth Section come all the way to America for this kind of mission?

"Strakhov?" Bolan shouted.

There was a silence, then another grating laugh.

"There is no way you could know that unless you are John Phoenix. Yes, I am Strakhov. I was the one who designed and engineered the attack on Stony Man Farm, and then again in Russia. You killed my son in Afghanistan. And today you are going to die for it.''

Bolan had brought the Childers around and slanted it down over the lip. He fired six shots at the cave entrance.

When the sound of the shots died away, he heard a groan and a sharp intake of breath.

After a pause the voice came again. ''Do not be excited, American. It is only a scratch. And by now my pilot will have retrieved the plans from the crash site and be flying away.''

''Wrong, Strakhov. I put six rounds into his engine. He won't last long. You're alone, you're almost out of ammunition and you're in the middle of the Mojave desert. You don't stand a chance.''

''You lie, John Phoenix. I know your style. I have studied you for three years. If my pilot had any problems he would tell me by radio, and I have lots of ammunition. Today you shall return to the ashes and there is no better place than this desert hell.''

17

The Executioner's mind was busy computing the odds, working on strategy. He had to find a way to flush the Russian out into the open.

Bolan shook his head to clear the sweat that was now coursing down his forehead into his eyes. Strakhov had eluded him before, but this time the KGB boss would not escape. The Executioner unslung the Childers and fired into the maze of rocks and the black hole. He was moving even before the sound of the second shot stopped echoing along the gulley.

Bolan stopped and checked his surroundings. There was considerable growth of hardy desert grass and a few smoke trees. Ground cover sage clung to the sides of the ravine, interspersed with a scattering of chaparral and greasewood. Bolan noticed that the grass, now dead, dry and fallen down, grew almost to the top of the ravine wall.

He squirmed back from the edge until he was out of sight, then scurried downstream ten yards to the grassy spot. He wormed back up to the lip of the gully and pulled out his cigarette lighter.

Carefully he reached over the drop-off and touched the flame to the grass. The tinder-dry vegetation caught fire as if it had been doused with gasoline. The flames exploded in the scrub and greasewood and whipped downwind, pushed by the breeze. There was nothing to stop it until it had passed the rock cavern and the jumble of boulders where Strakhov surely must be hiding. Then it would burn out.

The fire leaped, spread outward. A small flaming branch of sage blew ahead and started a spot fire a dozen yards forward of the main fire, which now had surged across the twenty-yard-wide gully.

Bolan pulled back from the edge and ran along the arroyo until he was just beyond the boulders, then crept up to the top of the drop-off and peered over the bank again. He put the M-16 on the ground and wiped sweat off his forehead. Then he thumbed wetness from both eyes and blinked. The smoke blew past the rocks, surging faster than the flames. He could see the wall of fire working toward the boulders.

Any time now there should be a rat running for his life. Bolan brought up the Childers. He was less than forty yards from the boulders. Strakhov would be ten to fifteen yards from him as he ran through the ravine. There was no way Bolan could miss with the shotgun.

Seconds ticked by and the Executioner waited. He thought he sensed some kind of movement to his left, but he could not risk pulling his eyes from the boulders to check. He would kill Strakhov now, the moment he ran out of the boulders, whether he was on fire or not. Strakhov would get all twelve rounds left in the Childers, and if the double ought buck did not do it, Bolan would use the M-16.

Movement near the rocks!

A shadow edged nearer the sunshine, then a figure burst out of the smoke, coughing and spluttering. Bolan started to lift the Childers when he heard a sound to his left. It was a sound that can reduce a strong man to a quivering mass of fear.

The chattering buzzing rattle of the snake's tail came again, harder, faster, more insistent this time. Bolan froze. He turned his eyes to the left without moving his head. He knew the creature was close. He saw it two feet from his left shoulder. A deadly Pacific rattlesnake had coiled on top of the warm black metal of the M-16, its tail a blur as it rattled its warning.

The serpent's liquid black eyes stared into Bolan's. Its tongue darted out, sensing the heat of the man, and catching the scent of smoke and heat coming toward it.

The Executioner knew he could not move. Nothing was faster than a coiled rattlesnake at two feet. His eyes pivoted back to the canyon. General Strakhov had raced from his lair out of the fire, looking behind him. He surged again, and now was opposite Bolan. He carried a Russian AK-47 with a thirty-round magazine. The Executioner felt fury and frustration drive through him as he saw his quarry slipping away.

He considered everything. His finger was still on the trigger of the Childers. The muzzle was pointing toward the gully, but not downward. Neither was it pointing at the snake. The creature continued to rattle, but the intensity was now reduced. Did that mean it was less frightened, that the warning had worked and now the snake was more at ease, less on its guard?

Bolan moved his eyes back so he could see the triangular head of the poisonous snake. The deadly fangs still wove a gentle pattern in front of the coiled power of its four-foot-long body. The rattler was as dangerous now as when Bolan first saw it.

The Executioner considered every possibility. Was he faster than the snake? Could he bring around his weapon rapidly enough to blast the reptile? Frustration gripped him as he thought of Strakhov escaping even as he pondered his plight. He felt he had no choice. He had to go for the rattler.

Lightning fast, the Executioner made his move. The Childers roared even before the muzzle acquired target. Five rounds of double ought buck ripped into the reptile, disintegrating the deadly head.

The snake's tail beat out a tattoo of rattling anger. Bolan sat up and looked at the creature. The headless body now lay uncoiled a few feet away from the M-16. Bolan grabbed the weapon.

The Executioner looked down the gully. Strakhov was nowhere in sight along the watercourse. Bolan ran down from the edge, checking the ravine every twenty feet. No Strakhov.

Bolan ran twenty yards farther, then moved slowly back up toward the drop-off to check. A rifle shot seared across his left thigh and he dived for cover in the ravine.

Strakhov! Bolan crawled slowly toward the gully lip. He scanned the terrain to his right where the shot had come from. Nothing. Movement in the shadow under an overhang? No. Strakhov must have gone farther.

Bolan realized he had to keep in range of the crashed chopper. He might have to give up on Strakhov if the blue and white helicopter headed for the plans to Operation Skysweeper. He slid down from the slope and ran upstream again. The depth of the watercourse lessened sharply, and soon it was only three feet deep. The Executioner found a spot behind a small sand dune and watched the gully.

After five minutes he saw movement, but Strakhov was almost a hundred yards away. Bolan sent a half dozen rounds after the Russian, then leaped up and ran for cover down from the edge of the arroyo.

He had gone only twenty yards when two rifle slugs slapped the sand near him and he dived behind another dune.

Bolan scowled. The gully was getting shallower here, giving neither of them much protection. He looked back at the crashed chopper. It was in sight, in range and safe. For a moment Bolan wondered if he would have a real shot at Strakhov. The Russian moved like a seasoned infantry soldier. Only if he made some big mistake would the Executioner have a chance for a kill.

Bolan followed as the Russian moved across the arid ground. Strakhov was working an arc around the downed chopper. Each time he tried to move toward it, Bolan drove him back with a shot or two.

The M-16 still had one 40mm grenade, but Strakhov was well out of its effective range.

The sweat came freely, bathing the Executioner's shirt, dripping off his nose. The sun burned into his skin. Nearly a half hour after they had begun playing cat and mouse in the furnace of a desert, Bolan heard a rotor throb, then saw the blue and white chopper approaching. The enemy bird circled once and then landed twenty yards from the KGB chief, but over a quarter of a mile away from Bolan and protected by a sand dune.

Bolan emptied a magazine at the piece of the bird he could see, then concentrated on Strakhov as he zigzagged toward the craft. The bullets plowed harmlessly into the sand. The Executioner sent another half a magazine of lead chargers after the helicopter as it took off.

Bolan took a long breath and watched in anger and frustration as the man he hated with all his being flew away free toward the south.

18

Bolan stood in the middle of the trackless Mojave desert watching the helicopter become a speck in the blue sky. Strakhov, the one man in the world Bolan wanted to kill more than any other, was escaping. He would trade one shot at Strakhov for a hundred other KGB agents! Bolan wished he had a radio so he could call in the Navy chopper.

Then he heard it, and turned to see the green Navy helicopter swinging in toward him. It settled down twenty yards away, sending up a sand and dust storm that Bolan fought his way through.

He jumped in the open passenger's side, strapped his seat belt and pointed upward.

When they were away from the dust, Bolan wiped the sweat and sand out of his eyes.

"You read minds too, Johnson?"

"You bet, sir. But I'm best at shadowing the other team's chopper. I guess you want me to keep on following that bird up there heading south?"?

"Damn right! On board is one of the top men in the KGB. Don't know how the hell he got into this country."

Ten minutes later, it became obvious that they were gaining on the other craft as it headed almost due south.

"We can catch them, but it'll take most of an hour."

"We've got to force them down! Can't we get any more speed out of this thing?"

"We're on the red line now, Mr. Scott."

Bolan stared at the blue and white craft. It swept around the end of the Sierra Nevadas, heading southwest.

"Where the hell is he going?" Bolan asked.

"My guess is a freighter or submarine outside the twelve-mile limit. No way we can even challenge them out there."

"Get on the horn and demand some Navy fighters to intercept that bird, force it down before it gets over the water."

"We can nail them before they get twelve miles out. I just figured it on my magic board here. We overtake them in thirty-six minutes."

"How far are we from the coast?"

"On this heading we're one hundred forty miles due southeast. We've been heading south to get around the hills. This new course puts us over the Pacific at Point Conception."

Something had been bothering Bolan. The plans, designs and secrets of Operation Skysweeper would be safe enough back in the desert in the middle of the huge Navy range. There was something else.

"Dr. Ludlow!"

"I tried to spot him when I was back there, but no way. I was too high."

"We have to go back."

"I thought you wanted that KGB general son of a bitch?"

"I do. Real bad. But I can't trade him for the top laser scientist in the world. We have to go back and find Dr. Ludlow before he dies in the heat."

"Have to, sir?"

"Turn it around, sailor, now!"

They made a wide sweep and roared back the other way. The Executioner looked at the vanishing blue and white chopper as the Navy pilot got on the radio, requested pursuit of Strakhov's chopper.

Bolan sat there gripping his shotgun. His knuckles showed white as he thought of Strakhov. So close! He had the butcher in his sights and once again the KGB chief eluded him. Damn!

The Executioner thought of the cold face, the eyes staring blankly up at him as they carried her away. Forever. Eternity. He would never see her again, never touch her again, never kiss her tender lips....

He had won the game, made all the right moves—and then the Mojave desert and its slithering denizen had conspired to nullify everything. One Pacific rattlesnake had outpointed both his weapons.

"Sir."

Bolan looked up. He was aware the young pilot had said it before.

"Sir, I got the base. Sent the request. They said they will need better authorization to force down a civilian chopper that we can't positively identify. Do we have any better federal authorization?"

"Tell them to contact Dr. Peterson. He's the biggest name I know they can refer to. I can't give them the authority."

Five minutes later they were hovering above the downed chopper. Johnson settled to the ground beside it and Bolan transferred the two boxes of paper, plans, graphs and test results to the Navy bird. Then they started a systematic quadrant search of the area around the downed chopper, looking for Dr. Roth Ludlow.

Bolan felt the moisture work through his shirt. He swiped at the sweat on his forehead. Twice he drank water from the canteen the pilot had brought along. There was also a five-gallon can of emergency water to the rear.

They searched one strip after another, working gradually away from the crash site.

Twice they thought they saw footprints in the sand, but by the time they got the glasses on them, the prints faded into the shadows and were nothing but ridges of sand.

For another hour they searched till they were well beyond the point where a human could walk across the burning sand. They went back to the base point at the wreckage and began combing the territory again, both men watching, knowing that time was fast running out for the man on the desert floor.

They were half a mile from the initial point when Bolan heard the sound of a slug whining off the body of the chopper.

"Down there!" Bolan shouted. "It has to be him. He's still got the Beretta. Go upwind of him and blow a dust storm his way. Then we can set down and I'll jump out."

They moved east so the rotorwash would pick

up the dust and carry it where the shot had originated. Slowly the hovering chopper descended as dust wheeled and eddied and blew toward the small dune.

The Executioner jumped out the door when the bird was two feet off the desert. He ducked and ran into the dust.

At once he was blinded. He could see only a few feet ahead. The chopper lifted off and as the dust thinned, he got his direction and ran forward.

Somewhere above the clatter of the aircraft's engine he heard three more shots. He hit the sand, waited, then moved more slowly in the direction of the sound. The dust and sand came again, cutting into him as the rotor blades kicked it up and slammed it westward. He ran with the sand now, heard the weapon fire again and he veered more to the left.

There was a pocket of clear air, and ahead ten yards he saw Dr. Ludlow. His shirt was off, his head and torso were burned bright red. The scientist held one hand over his eyes and fired the Beretta straight into the sky.

Bolan charged forward, slapped the Beretta out of the scientist's hand and grabbed him.

Ludlow struggled vainly against the iron grip of the Executioner. The desert heat and lack of water finally sapped the physicist's strength and he fell limply into Bolan's arms.

The Executioner wiped sand from Dr. Ludlow's feverish face.

"Dr. Ludlow. It's all right. Everything is fine. It's all over. We're going back to the center."

Heavy-lidded eyes, swollen and burned, tried to blink. Ludlow shivered and then his eyes relaxed, his head rolled forward. He was unconscious.

The Executioner stuffed the Beretta into his waistband, picked up the big scientist and carried him over his shoulder to the chopper.

Bolan and the pilot helped Dr. Ludlow into the chopper and they took off for the base. They gave him a sip of water and a wet cloth he could suck on. Slowly he came around and soon insisted that they tell him what happened.

The Executioner explained everything that had happened up to that point.

"We figured it was some kind of posthypnotic suggestion they planted in you at the Hanoi Hilton," Bolan said. "But the only way we could find the higher contacts was to let you take the material and meet them."

Dr. Ludlow scowled. "So our big 'escape' in Nam was planned. They released us close enough to our own lines so we couldn't get lost. I'll be damned. They brainwashed us, planted these post-hypnotics and let us go."

He told them about the mind flashes, the Delayed Stress Syndrome. Simply a new name for battle fatigue.

Bolan asked him about Skysweeper.

"It never will be totally complete. But this phase of it is certainly over. We've done everything we started out to do. When we first shot a laser beam at the moon we were thrilled that it was only two miles wide where it hit. Now we're trying to get that dispersion cut down to a foot wide at ten thousand miles. Research will go on. The better we get, the better the laser will be and the more powerful and potent our weapons. But for now, it's at a leveling-off spot.''

Then Dr. Ludlow looked at Bolan again.

"I'm not sure we've met. I don't understand your exact duties on our program.''

"Dr. Peterson can fill you in on the details.''

Bolan cleared the shotgun and the M-16 and put them in the duffel bag.

"Lieutenant Johnson, any developments on those chase planes?''

Johnson called the tower at Armitage Field. He listened on the earphones, then signed off.

"They scrambled two Air Force jets to intercept the craft on that heading, but they had no reason and no authority to interfere with its flight. They followed the chopper over the coastline at Point Conception, and about fifteen miles off the coast the chopper landed on board a freighter flying a Soviet flag. The NC number of the civilian helicopter was noted and its owner will be contacted. The Air Force pilots reported that the chopper was being lashed down as they broke contact and returned to base. It looked like the bird was set for a long trip.''

The Executioner scowled. "Figures,'' he said.

DR. PETERSON WAS AT THE FIELD to meet the chopper when it landed. He had brought Dr. Ludlow's car and supervised the transfer of the top-secret documents to the vehicle. Then he rode with them back to the big safe.

An ambulance met them at the field too. Despite his protests it took Dr. Ludlow to the branch clinic for observation.

Bolan's rented Ford sat near the landing site. He took the green barracks bag and stowed it in the trunk. In his billfold he found the list of phone numbers he had taken from the Smith safe. He drove out the airfield security gate and back to the women officers' quarters.

At a phone booth he called Malia's number. She answered on the first ring.

"Yes?"

"Malia, this is Mack."

"Oh! I'm glad you called! What's been happening?"

"I'll explain everything over lunch. Meet you in ten minutes." Bolan hung up, then called Dr. Peterson's office.

"Everything back in the right place and safe?"

"Yes. And Kara is in custody."

"You should have the rest of the phone numbers and corral a few more." He gave Dr. Peterson the numbers. "You might also want to raid that safehouse where they held Dr. Ludlow. And call his wife that he is safe and well."

"We've notified Mrs. Ludlow." There was a pause at the other end. "Mack, there is no way on earth I can thank you. Both personally and for saving the Skysweeper project."

"No thanks necessary," Bolan said. "I won't be seeing you again, Dr. Peterson. Good luck."

Bolan drove to the women's quarters where Malia was waiting outside for him. He told her she could move the rest of her things out of the Smith house.

An hour later Bolan and the DIA agent entered the room at the Desert Inn Spa at the edge of town. She put down the small suitcase that she had retrieved from the Smith house and eyed the king-size water bed.

"Make yourself comfortable. I'm going to take a long shower," Bolan said.

Fifteen minutes later he came out of the bathroom with a towel wrapped around his middle, sarong-style.

Malia turned away from the window when she heard him padding into the room. She spread her arms wide, the movement taking in the fake fireplace, large bath with twin sinks and dressing area, small wet bar to one side. The whole thing was done in soft pastels with a two-inch-thick luxurious carpet on the floor.

"You know, I could get used to this."

"Why don't you give it a try for a week or so?"

She turned quickly. "You are going to need some twenty-four-hour nursing, I mean to get that bullet crease healed and that sunburn looked at."

They moved to the bed, then she turned toward him and slowly reached up and kissed his lips.

"Been wanting to do that for a long time, days."

His arms came around her and he tried to relax. It was going to take some time. Dr. Peterson would tie up the last loose ends, and Skysweeper was safe. Peterson was off the Russian hook, at least for now.

Malia twisted around in his arms and leaned her back against him. Then she sighed.

"Yes, I could get used to all of this," she repeated.

Bolan knew he could, too. But in three or four days he would move on, find a new spot where he could strike back at the hydra, where he could cut off another one of its insidious arms of evil. Every small victory counted, and perhaps some day down the road, he would have another chance at Strakhov, the KGB monster whom Mack Bolan had vowed to wipe off the face of the earth.

"Fortune smiled on you today, Strakhov. Next time you won't be so lucky." Bolan formed the words in his mind but he did not speak them. They were private.

A Brief History of
Mack Bolan's Military Career

Where did Mack Bolan learn his personal style of relentless warfare that allowed him to infiltrate a Mafia stronghold, destroy it, then simply retreat, leaving the feared and seemingly invincible Mob families reeling in confusion?

Vietnam. That Asian hellground spawned the menacing specter known throughout the world as The Executioner.

Bolan enlisted in the service at the age of eighteen. During his first tour of duty, he was stationed in three different countries—Korea, Germany and France—and rose rapidly through the ranks. He went to Vietnam as a sergeant under the command of Colonel James Crawford. Bolan became the consummate soldier, who could give as well as take orders.

When Crawford was rotated back to the U.S. he was replaced by Colonel Harlan Winters. Bolan and Winters became close friends despite their difference in rank. In fact, "Howlin'" Harlan Winters was the creator of the penetration teams, the father of Able Team.

The first Able Team mission involved Bolan, Colonel Winters, with five Montagnard tribesmen for support. After its initial success, the members of the team changed. "Whispering Death" Zitka joined Bolan as a flanker. Later, "Chopper" Fontenelli, "Boom-Boom" Hoffower, "Bloodbrother" Loudelk, "Flower Child" Andromede, "Gadgets" Schwarz, "Gunsmoke" Harrington and "Politician" Blancanales all worked with Bolan to become one of the deadliest forces in the Vietnam War.

In the Asian theater, Bolan met many large warriors: Wilson Brown, Bob McFee, Charles Rosky and Frank Harrelson. There were men like Jim Brantzen and Bruno Tassily, soldiers who warred on death as doctors to keep the troops alive.

There were others, sure. But not always warriors. In Nam Bolan also encountered "The Desert Rats," three men of a Green Beret A-team. Floyd Worthy, Jim Hinshaw and Angel Morales joined the U.S. Army only to escape the hot breath of the law. They took their erring ways to the jungles of Vietnam and used the war as a means of profiteering.

The trio instituted a campaign of terror and intimidation against the inhabitants of the region. Civilians were forced to pay "insurance" premiums or face arrest on charges of collusion with the Communists. Those who did not comply also paid—with their lives.

Bolan and his flanker, T. L. Minnegas, caught "The Desert Rats" in the act of executing three unarmed villagers. Bolan's intervention resulted in the indictment of Worthy, Morales and Hinshaw. The three killers were given dishonorable discharges from the service. Bolan had no way of knowing that his own military career was about to end and that he'd cross paths with the ruthless trio in years to come.

During the Southeast Asian conflict, Bolan had been recommended many times for promotions, but he turned them all down. An entry in his journal explains the reasons for his refusal:

> I don't want a promotion. It isn't that I can't handle the responsibility—I can. My place is out on the firing line, helping these war torn people. I cannot turn my back on the innocents struggling for survival when the VC savages are eating them whole. I would be less of a man if I did. War *is* hell. But I have a duty.

Then tragedy struck. Bolan was informed of the death of his parents and sister and the critical condition of his younger brother, all victims of Mafia violence. Sergeant Bolan was granted emergency leave to bury his family. He had four months remaining in his third tour of duty. The tour would never be completed.

The Executioner took the next step toward his destiny and entered the second phase of his colorful if blood-filled career. Bolan declared war on the Mafia. "I am not their judge or jury. I am their judgment! I am The Executioner."

This new enemy would prove to be every bit as savage as the animals he had fought in Nam.

DON PENDLETON'S EXECUTIONER
MACK BOLAN

Sergeant Mercy in Nam... The Executioner in the Mafia Wars... Colonel John Phoenix in the Terrorist Wars.... Now Mack Bolan fights his loneliest war! You've never read writing like this before. Faceless dogsoldiers have killed April Rose. The Executioner's one link with compassion is broken. His path is clear: by fire and maneuver, he will rack up hell in a world shock-tilted by terror. Bolan wages unsanctioned war—everywhere!

Available wherever paperbacks are sold.

GOLD EAGLE

**Nile Barrabas and the
Soldiers of Barrabas are the**

SOBs

by Jack Hild

Nile Barrabas is a nervy son of a bitch who was the last
American soldier out of Vietnam and the first man into a
new kind of action. His warriors, called the Soldiers of
Barrabas, have one very simple ambition: to do what the
Marines can't or won't do. Join the Barrabas blitz! Each
book hits new heights—this is brawling at its best!

"Nile Barrabas is one tough SOB himself.... A wealth
of detail.... SOBs does the job!"

—*West Coast Review of Books*

#1 **The Barrabas Run**   #3 **Butchers of Eden**
#2 **The Plains of Fire**   #4 **Gulag War**

HE'S EXPLOSIVE.
E'S MACK BOLA ...
AGAINST ALL ODDS

He learned his deadly skills in Vietnam...then put them to good use by destroying the Mafia in a blazing one-man war. Now **Mack Bolan** ventures further into the cold to take on his deadliest challenge yet—the KGB's worldwide terror machine.

Follow the lone warrior on his exciting new missions...and get ready for more nonstop action from his high-powered combat teams: **Able Team**—Bolan's famous Death Squad—battling urban savagery too brutal and volatile for regular law enforcement. And **Phoenix Force**—five extraordinary warriors handpicked by Bolan to fight the dirtiest of antiterrorist wars, blazing into even greater danger.

Fight alongside these three courageous forces for freedom in all-new action-packed novels! Travel to the gloomy depths of the cold Atlantic, the scorching sands of the Sahara, and the desolate Russian plains. You'll feel the pressure and excitement building page after page, with nonstop action that keeps you enthralled until the explosive conclusion!

Now you can have all the new Gold Eagle novels delivered right to your home!

You won't want to miss a single one of these exciting new action-adventures. And you don't have to! Just fill out and mail the card at right, and we'll enter your name in the Gold Eagle home subscription plan. You'll then receive six brand-new action-packed Gold Eagle books every other month, delivered right to your home! You'll get two Mack Bolan novels, one Able Team and one Phoenix Force, plus one book each from two thrilling, new Gold Eagle libraries, **SOBs** and **Track**. In **SOBs** you'll meet the legendary team of mercenary warriors who fight for justice and win. **Track** features a military and weapons genius on a mission to stop a maniac whose dream is everybody's worst nightmare. Only Track stands between us and nuclear hell!

FREE! <u>The New War Book</u> and Mack Bolan bumper sticker.

As soon as we receive your card we'll rush you the long-awaited <u>New War Book</u> and Mack Bolan bumper sticker—both ABSOLUTELY FREE. Then under separate cover, you'll receive your six Gold Eagle novels.

<u>The New War Book</u> is *packed* with exciting information for Bolan fans: a revealing look at the hero's life...two new short stories...book character biographies...even a combat catalog describing weapons used in the novels! <u>The New War Book</u> is a special collector's item you'll want to read again and again. And it's yours FREE when you mail your card!

Of course, you're under no obligation to buy anything. Your first six books come on a 10-day free trial—if you're not thrilled with them, just return them and owe nothing. <u>The New War Book</u> and bumper sticker are yours to keep, FREE!

Don't miss a single one of these thrilling novels...mail the card now, while you're thinking about it.

JOIN FORCES WITH MACK BOLAN AND HIS NEW COMBAT TEAMS!

Mail this coupon today!